ELEMENTAL WITCH

THE QUESTING WITCH SERIES, BOOK 4

SHANNON MAYER

HiJinks

Elemental Witch
Questing Witch Series Book 4
Shannon Mayer

My name is Pamela, and I am the strongest witch the world has ever seen.

Only I'm not just a witch. I'm an elemental, and that truth makes me a target and a threat.

The elementals of this world are done hiding in the shadows. And a faction of them want to rule our world. They want to put the humans under their heels, and they want all the power to themselves.

Standing between them and their goal are only two people, two who still hold a connection to Spirit, the key to stopping them. Myself and my father.

But the elementals we face are no fools. And they've taken the most precious thing from us both.

A child who is everything they need to force all creation to bend knee. A child who I've always known was special.

They've taken Frost.

And if I have to break the world again to find him, I will.

Because I'm done hiding too.

And the elementals had better be ready to play.

HiJinks Ink Publishing
www.shannonmayer.com

Original illustrations by Ravven
Photography by With Love Photography
Mayer, Shannon

❀ Created with Vellum

ACKNOWLEDGMENTS

This one is for all those who struggle with their own
darkness, whatever form that darkness may come in.
Don't ever forget that you are loved, by more people than
you realize.
Don't ever forget that you are stronger than you know.
Don't you dare ever give up.

For my little sister.

PAMELA

The dark of the night weighed on me as though I had an entire mountain pressing on my shoulders, the rock and age of it working to pin me to the bottom of the ravine I stood in. Gritting my teeth against the feeling, I forced my feet to walk, to move forward, to throw off that heavy sensation. I couldn't give in to the pressure—I had to do what was right. No matter of the choices in front of me.

Frost was missing. The elementals had taken him, and I had to find him before they did something horrible. But I had to stay here, with the Caravan, waiting for Raven to be ready to go after Frost. To wait, when all you wanted was to move, that was the worst part.

What if the elementals hurt him? What if they killed him? My thoughts were rampant with all the possibilities. None which put my mind or heart at ease.

Oka walked with me. My truest friend, the one soul I could always count on, my familiar—and currently a small house cat rather than her larger tiger form. Her peachy orange fur caught the starlight as she trotted alongside. "You didn't tell Richard, did you?"

Her question made me grimace. Richard was the leader of the caravan I'd sworn to protect. He didn't know what I was about to do. That I was going to leave him and the caravan to look for Frost. It would leave the caravan without protection, but with the first witch locked away, they were safer than they had ever been.

"Dick doesn't need to worry. Raven is helping him with that," I said.

Oka snorted. "Raven . . . I know he's your father—"

"He helped me save you." I cut her off, my eyes tracking the movement of the stream ahead. "And I understand why he's done terrible things in the hopes of making this world better. The choices aren't always easy, Oka. Sometimes there is no good answer, and someone must make that hard decision. Sometimes . . . people don't know you're the hero until they've already condemned you as a villain."

She sighed. "I was only going to say that you don't know everything about why the elementals took your brother. There could be something more than what Raven is telling you. Raven could have done something to anger them. Even you can't argue with that logic. Not that it makes it okay to take the boy."

My stomach rolled, sour with anxiety, because she wasn't wrong. "I know. That's why I can't stand still." I shivered, and that weight to the air tugged at me again. Bloody hell, I wanted to run away from this, but I was not a child.

The elementals didn't like that I was a "mutt," born of

Raven, a powerful elemental, and my mother, a powerful witch. They'd tried to bind my power from me, and when that failed, tried to kill me. That hadn't worked either, and now they'd taken Frost. Was it bait to draw me in? If so, then it would work very well. I would go to the ends of the earth for him.

Frost, the little boy I'd been so drawn to from the moment I'd come to this caravan, had turned out to be my half-brother, born of Samara, a powerful Sylph. It made me wonder if I had any other half-siblings. How many of us were out there? A shock to be sure, but also a feeling of "ah, there's the missing piece" had hit me when Raven told me.

Oka and I were at the stream now and I held my hand over it, feeling my ability to control the water just under my skin. I flexed my fingers and a tiny spurt of liquid flowed upward. I flattened it out with a few quick flicks of my fingers until it was a mirror.

From the moment I'd stepped out of the maze of the first witch, I'd been forced to keep moving forward, to not look back, to not fear what had happened in what was not really a maze, but the Veil. A feeling of being chased had my feet pacing the stream up and down, over and over. I couldn't remain in one spot.

Standing still would be the worst thing I could do. I didn't even fully understand why that was so true in my head, but it was.

I'd healed the rips that Alex and I had put into the Veil three years ago, healed the wounds that had torn the world apart. But that wouldn't put the rest of what had happened back together—there would be no making time flow backward. I stared in the water's reflection at myself, at the lines of my face, at the blue eyes that were just like my father's, and just like Frost's, really. My hair was darker than his, a deep golden, and more than that . . . I touched a spot just in front of my left ear. Silvery white strands flowed where they'd been golden the last I'd seen.

"Oka, what is happening to me?" I touched the silvery tones; it was not my familiar who answered, but the magic that connected me to my mother's bloodlines.

Magical trauma will cause outward changes . . . that and you wove the dark and the light like a master witch. That will leave its mark on you for all to see. You are growing stronger. That's good. I think you're going to need to be stronger than you've ever been before. If I didn't know better, she sounded tired.

Sam's voice was not as harsh as it had once been. While it had taken me a long time to realize that dark didn't necessarily mean evil, I was still wary. Sam—the name I'd given the magic—could be tricky, and I had to remain on my toes around her. Even if she *was* a part of me. Even if we'd worked together to survive the First Witch.

I waved my hand, cutting it through the water mirror, displacing the droplets in all directions. Oka grumbled and stepped back, shaking her head as the water dripped on her fur. "What is Raven doing exactly?"

"Making Richard and the others believe that Frost and I have gone on ahead to find the Haven. He's telling them not to worry, not to look for us."

I didn't need to see Oka's eyebrows climb to feel her question his methods.

"He's using spirit to bend their memories." She didn't say it like she was asking a question. She didn't have to. We both knew what Raven was capable of. He was my father, yes, but I knew him, and I was not surprised by how far he would go to make things happen the way he saw fit.

Worse, I understood his actions more the older I got. He'd once told me that someone had to make the hard decisions, and I'd thought he was making an excuse for himself and his actions. Now, though . . . those hard decisions were becoming mine.

I was facing choices I didn't want to, that would shape the world around me.

"As far as I know that is what he's doing." I turned and walked downstream, my mind disconnected from this place I stood in. I'd come out of the maze, no, the Veil, that morning. Injured and broken from my battle with the First Witch. I'd not cared as much about the physical damages as the new wounds that had scarred my heart.

Mac's blue eyes would haunt me the rest of my days. I knew that through and through. He'd loved me truly, and I him. Losing him . . . was like losing a connection to the good in this world. I swallowed hard, my throat thick and tight with the need to cry, and the inability to do so. There wasn't time. There was never time to grieve properly, and Mac deserved to be grieved.

Forcing my mind away from him, from the loss of his love and how he'd grounded me, I tried to concentrate on what had been done, and what still lay ahead. I'd put the First Witch inside an oubliette and trapped her there, seeing as everyone said she couldn't be killed. Part of me wished I'd tried to end her life, because as sure as the sun rose in the east, I did not doubt for a second that she wasn't finished trying to make her way in this world.

The other part of me was smart enough to know a powerhouse when she saw it. The First Witch had more power in her than I could possibly face, more tricks up her sleeve than if I had a hundred years to practice my magic. It was only the fact that she'd underestimated me that I'd been able to pin her down. Or maybe she hadn't underestimated me exactly. No doubt she'd thought I'd just rely purely on my magic, and not my mind or body.

Rubbing my hands up and down my arms, the tingle in my palms reminded me that I'd been so close to losing to the First Witch. Sheer luck had allowed me to escape.

I shook my head and kept walking. Oka continued to pace alongside me. "And Alex, did you tell him that we are leaving?"

My throat tightened further, and I said nothing. I didn't know what to say. That it was complicated talking to Alex now? Because I loved him, my heart had always loved him, and now with Mac gone, in theory, I could follow that love if I wanted, but that I was scared? That losing Mac, the second man I'd loved and lost, had me reeling and afraid to be around anyone else I cared for?

"Second man?" Oka asked softly, picking up on my thoughts as she did from time to time. "You never told me about anyone else."

I pulled in a shuddering breath and picked through my memories for a moment before speaking, seeing the young man who'd been my first kiss, who'd been the first one to make my heart beat faster. "Before the rending of the world, there was a young necromancer. His name was Frank. He saved me, and he was my first love that I realized was my first love. He died protecting me." Just like Mac had died to keep me out of the First Witch's hands.

A series of tremors began in my feet and rumbled their way up my legs and through my body until I had to stop walking. But that was not good, I needed to keep moving. I felt that in the center of my bones.

For years, I'd closed myself from my emotions, from feeling anything more than anger, and going through the Veil had shown me how very foolish that had been. Only now that I'd been cracked open, I felt everything a thousand times over, and the pieces of my life looked like the shards of a broken mirror, and as sharp in my soul. There was a reason, I was sure, but I didn't want to think about that right now. I just wanted to pretend it was all done, and that I wasn't hurting like this, feeling everything as though a dam had broken.

Oka shifted into her tiger form and I leaned against her, letting her help me stand. "Oka, promise me that you will not do the same. I . . . don't think I could survive if I lost you too." Even as I spoke the words, my heart hammered uncomfortably in my chest as though it would run away if it could. Was I really worried she'd leave me? No, she would never do that, but the fear was still there.

I dug my fingers deep into the thick fur of her stripeless dark orange coat. She let out a rumble and bumped her big head against me. "Don't talk about that right now. You have to focus on the task at hand, not the fears of what could be. And I will never leave you, no matter what comes. There is nothing you could do or say that would take me from you."

I drew in a shaking breath before I spoke. "You sound like Peta."

"Good, she's much better at this sort of thing than me. And I am trying to be like her." She butted her head against my side.

"I don't need Peta. I need you. What would you say?" I asked.

"Stop fussing over old shit; it still stinks, but only if you keep stepping back in it."

A laugh caught me off guard, because the day had been nothing but dark and pain and grief. I clung to her, bent my head and buried my nose in her thick fur. "Oka, never, ever change. Don't try to be Peta. She is amazing, but you are damn well brilliant. And right."

Even so, that didn't mean I wasn't able to grieve for Mac. For all that he was, all that I'd thought we'd have together, and now all that was lost. He would be mourned. Just not right then.

"You still didn't tell me what you planned on saying to Alex," Oka said. Her left ear flicked. "Too late."

Too late?

The wind swept up behind me, bringing me the lightest smell of wolf. I was no shifter, but even with my nose, I could smell Alex. Sweat, blood, and wolf. It was a combination that needed a serious shower.

I half turned, my hands still hanging onto Oka.

Alex was about ten feet behind us, his golden eyes glowing in the dark. "Where are you going, Pam?"

"To find Frost," I said. "He's my brother."

Alex didn't close the distance between us like he would have in the past. I swallowed hard, feeling that pain of separation once more. "Oka told me that you inherited your father's abilities. That you're an incubus now."

He closed his eyes, the golden orbs going dark for a long moment, before he opened them again. "I did. I'm not particularly good at controlling it yet."

A tired smile crept across my face. "Tell me about it."

Hey, don't be comparing me to an incubus and his powers. Sam was indignant, but I ignored her. For now, anyway.

"I'm coming with you," he said. "With Mac gone, you need someone to protect you. You have a knack, you know, for finding trouble." He smiled, a quirk of his lips, and his face softened with a look I knew too well. Love, he loved me.

People who loved me died.

Push him away. You have to push him away. His love will kill you in the end. That was not Sam, but my own thoughts.

"She has a protector." Raven's voice cut through the darkness, disembodied. It took me a moment to find him, dressed all in black from his boots to his cloak, to the blue-black of his hair. His cloak was pulled up high, hiding his face as if he were indeed the villain I'd just compared him to. "She does not need you, incubus. You would drain her without meaning to, no matter how you feel about her."

His words felt like a slap to me, and apparently to Alex too. He let out a low growl and the scent of wolf sharpened in the air.

9

Oka grunted. "Stupid men. Raven, we are going up against many elementals, yes?"

Raven turned to face us. "Yes, at the least of what lies ahead."

At the least? What else were we going to be facing?

"Then are we not better to just take him with us? The elementals can be drained by an incubus as surely as any other supernatural," Oka said. "That is not something they will expect. I cannot believe that you would leave behind such a valuable tool."

To say I was surprised that Oka would face Raven over bringing Alex was a bit of an understatement. Not that I minded, but prior to me coming out of the Veil, there had been more than a little animosity between Alex and my tiger. The whole *cats rule and dogs drool* line had been tossed around more than once between them.

And the fact that she referred to Alex as a tool was not lost on me, nor the fact that he didn't react to her wording. In fact, he gave a subtle nod in her direction, a thank-you for speaking up for him; she returned it, just as subtle.

From Oka, I had the distinct impression that she was serious, and not inclined to leave Alex behind. Whatever had happened between them while I'd been in the maze had bonded them far stronger than I'd realized. A tiny spurt of uncertainty flared through me. What kind of connection did they have now?

Raven looked at me from under the cowl of his hood. "His life will be in great danger, Pamela. Can you allow yourself to let him risk it once more? To lose another person you love?"

Images of Mac dying in my arms, and of young Frank

dying for me, hit me like a runaway horse, bowling me over and stomping what was left of my uncertainty into the ground.

Damn my father for knowing how to manipulate me, and for his words to echo my own thoughts from only moments before. He wasn't wrong. "No, I won't let him do that. I'm sorry, Alex, but this is goodbye." I hadn't meant to say that last bit, but it flowed out of me anyway. And I knew it was the truth. This was goodbye. I couldn't be with him. I couldn't love him the way we both wanted.

It was better this way, a clean cut.

I took two steps toward Raven and held out my hand while still touching Oka. Raven's fingers curled around my wrist as he wove spirit and used it to jump the Veil, leaving Alex and the caravan behind, away from me.

Where they were safe.

Even if it tore out the last pieces of my heart.

2

ALEX

"Damn it, Pam, no!" I reached for the edge of her cloak in that split second before she disappeared from my life yet again.

I thought I'd caught hold of her, I was sure I'd felt the soft brush of the material against my fingertips, but the sensation was there and gone in an instant and I was left standing alone next to the little stream with nothing but the night noises for my companions. A snarl of frustration blew out of me before I could catch it. I paced the bank of the burbling waters as I tried to work out what to do next.

Did I go after her? Did I stay?

I loved her still. I always would and I knew that no matter how much space was between us, the truth was there—she was my Pam. She was my girl and even if she didn't ever love me the way I loved her, I would always be her friend. I knew she needed time to heal from losing Mac, and that was going to be a road I couldn't walk with her. Another sigh slid from me, less angry and more resigned as I knew what I had to do. I'd waited for her this long; I could wait a little longer, however long it took. But even waiting, I wanted to help her, to protect her from the trials she was going to face.

The soft pad of a big cat's footsteps stopped me in my pacing. "Bad night?" A voice from my past spoke softly.

I did a slow turn to see a spotted snow leopard watching me from the far side of the stream. Her green eyes glowed, catching the light of the moon here and there. But I wasn't really sure that what I was seeing was what I was seeing. "Peta?"

"The one and only. The Mother Goddess has assigned me to look out for you. At least for a little bit." She gave a jaw-cracking yawn. "It seems you've lost the girls again."

I grimaced and those jeweled green eyes never left my face. "Perhaps they are not meant to be with you, Alex. Perhaps it is time that you realize that Pamela's path is not yours. It never has been."

"I don't know that *lost* is the right word." I couldn't help but stare at the snow leopard. She had died. I knew that much. But really then, how could she be here?

Peta tipped her head, one ear flicking as she answered my unspoken question. "The Veil has been healed, and so the spirits of those who are sworn guardians of the world can walk freely again. The First Witch did some terrible damage, trapping many of us when she woke and began to use the dead to her advantage. Close your jaw, unless you plan on catching bugs."

My jaw snapped shut. Of course, that made some sense, but I hadn't realized all that. Pamela likely knew, but we'd not had even a moment to catch up. She'd been healed by her father, then she'd avoided me the rest of the day. Raven had done something to the memories of those in the caravan and when he'd approached me, I'd slipped away.

"So what, o great spotted cat, do you suggest I do?" I asked, no small amount of irritation in my voice.

Her laughter was low. "I like that. Great Spotted Cat. You wait for the moment you will be needed, Oh Horny Wolf pup." She winked an eye at me and even in the cool of the night my skin flamed hot.

"I'm *not* horny. I'm an incubus; there is a difference."

"Perhaps, but if you are going to tease me, do not expect me to go lightly on you."

I swear one of her eyebrows raised. I lifted both hands in mock surrender. "Fine, I'm a fucking werewolf, I get it."

Her laughter rang out loud across the water, and she padded closer to me. "That *is* funny, Alex. Incubus and shifter, you are indeed that."

"I thought to tell Oka that one." I sighed, my shoulders drooping.

"She is bonded to you too, yes? I sensed it between you and her before she flitted away." Peta did raise an brow then.

"I think so, like a pack member." I nodded.

"That will save her." Peta's eyes closed and she scented the air, nostrils flaring. "You will save Oka, and it will break her heart all in one fell swoop."

"I don't like the sound of that."

"No, I do not either." Peta shook her head. "I wish I could see further than that for you, Alex, but I cannot."

The sounds of feet and the squeak of plastic turned my head. Marley ran toward me, her brown hair a mess of knots and her face flushed in the moonlight, her water-proof coat squeaking as she hurried toward me.

"Alex, what are you doing up still?"

I snorted. "From the thirteen-year-old who's up past midnight?"

She shrugged. "Everyone is still awake. Sad about Pam and Frost leaving, you know. But they'll find the Haven and then we'll all be safe!"

I bit my lower lip to keep from snarling at the lie. So that's what Raven had people thinking, that Pam had taken Frost? I couldn't help but prod at the lie she'd been fed. "Why did she take him, again?"

"Well, he was sick. She thought there was a healer up ahead? In the Haven. I think?" Marley frowned as if the lie embedded in her head didn't quite sit right with her any more than it sat with me. "I think?" She repeated those two words softly as she rubbed at her head.

I put an arm around her shoulder and tucked her into my side. Funny enough, the incubus powers in me were silent, not making even a peep of wanting to take Marley's life.

Peta watched us, once more answering me as if she were in my head. "I think it is because she is part of your pack. You are there to protect her, and that is enough to keep it quiet. Oka would be the same . . . but Pamela, I doubt. She is not truly part of your pack, Alex."

I nodded but said nothing. I didn't want Marley thinking I was losing my marbles so soon after everything that had happened.

"Are you going to go after them?" Marley asked softly.

"I don't want you to go again. Not if you're going to leave me with Jasmine."

Shit. I hadn't told her about Jasmine. I swallowed hard. "Jasmine didn't make it. She won't watch over you ever again."

Marley slumped against me, and at first, I thought it was grief, and then realized it was relief. "I feel bad," she whispered, "for being glad that she's gone. I hope she didn't suffer, I guess."

My stomach rolled with the truth of how Jasmine had died, arching in my arms, her life sucked down into my belly. "No, she didn't suffer." She'd died smiling, thinking I loved her, thinking that I was going to keep her safe. My stomach rolled again, harder this time, and I had to clench my jaw to keep everything inside.

"That's good." Marley pulled away from me a little and looked up. "But you're still going after Pamela, aren't you?"

I wanted to, gods did I ever. Standing there, I could pinpoint Oka far to the south, thousands of miles was my guess, and where she was, Pam was. So in theory, I could go after them. But Pamela . . . didn't want me with her right now, and I had to let her grieve her way without forcing myself on her. This was one of those decisions I didn't want to make, because the right choice was not what I wanted. "No, I'm going to stay here. I'm going to watch over the caravan and you."

"Good choice," Peta said. "Because they are going to need you here. And Pamela needs you to stay here with them, at least for now. You'll know when to part ways with the caravan . . . when you find the big trees."

Before I could ask her what she meant, she turned, took a step, and disappeared as if she'd never been standing on the banks of the stream talking to me.

Above us, the sky rumbled. I looked up as clouds swept in, covering the stars and darkening the night further. I lifted my nose and breathed in the fresh new breeze. Marley mimicked me.

"That smells like rain," she said.

"Yeah, it does." This was what I was worried about. "Come on, let's go."

With my arm still around Marley's shoulder, I headed back toward the caravan proper. Voices swelled and dipped, laughter here and there even this late at night. Mostly the shifters by the sounds of it, but a few humans were still awake too.

The caravan had set up solidly inside the ravine, with a main larger fire that was kept going through the night, tents and lean-tos set up around it in a circle. More and more, they looked like they planned on staying long term. Which wasn't good given that the ravine was both a protection and a danger. I gave Marley a one-armed squeeze. "Go to bed, Mar. We're going to start out early tomorrow."

She wrapped her arms around me and hugged my middle. "Okay. Goodnight, Alex."

I watched her go, making sure she did as I asked, but I didn't really need to. She was a good kid, not a rebellious bone in her body. I wondered how that would affect her as she got older in this hard world. I wanted to protect her and keep her safe, but I knew it would only last so long.

Speaking of keeping her safe, there was a man I needed to speak to if I was going to help here, if I was going to look out for the caravan while Pamela was gone. I made my way past the small groups of people talking near the fire, and headed straight for the caravan leader, Richard.

He saw me coming and motioned for me to join him. "Alex, glad to see you didn't run off with Pam." His face crinkled into a frown. "Without her, the group doesn't want to move. Fear of the dead lands, and the potential monsters out there are going to make them want to stay here until she gets back. Which isn't a bad idea; this place is safe, like a fortress with the big walls." He motioned to the walls of the ravine.

That wasn't good. Time to grab the bull by the horns and shake him good. "We need to move in the morning," I said. "Rain is coming, and this is a bad place to be if we end up with a deluge, flood, or any serious amount of water. We'll be trapped. Those walls will become our death, instead of protection."

Richard spluttered. "Didn't you hear—"

"The Haven is to the east, right? And that's the direction that Pamela took with Frost." That lie was rancid on my tongue but I said it anyway. I sat beside him. "The more we sit here in the easy time of the summer, the more chance we have of being trapped come winter. The stream is low now, but as soon as the big rains come—and we're about to get some water—there is a high chance this entire ravine will flood. But if we go in the same direction as Pamela and Frost, then when they are coming back, we'll meet up with them even sooner." All around us the talk died down as people leaned in to hear what I was saying. Going after Pamela might have been what I wanted, but the people here needed someone to kick them into high gear and get them moving. Honestly, why did I have to work so hard to show him the logic of getting out of here?

Sitting still in this world was more dangerous than moving—by a very long shot.

I didn't look at anyone but Richard. "We should go in the morning, trust me when I say rain is coming. It's going to be a job to get the bigger vehicles out of here, probably take most of the day if the ravine edges turn to mud—which they will when the water hits the dry ground. My suggestion is we send one of the bird shifters ahead with Crimson to suss out the land directly to the east and find us a solid path. The rest of us will work to get the vehicles out by the end of the day." Even if it rained hard, we'd have time with the size of the ravine.

"We're safe here," a woman said. Chris, if I remembered right. She put a hand on Richard's shoulder. "Isn't that more important? To allow us to rest and be safe? It's what's best for the children, to have a place where they can feel safe."

I looked at her, wondered just how far I could push this. I seemed to remember Chris being a pain in Pamela's ass. Seemed like it was a place the woman liked to be.

"We won't be safe here for long," a new voice said. I turned as Wade stepped up. "There are elementals on the land now, roaming freely, and they are not all kind. Many of them are looking for slaves. Human slaves. Shifter slaves."

A series of gasps went up around the fire. I nodded to Wade, a silent thanks. We needed to move, and move as soon as we could—I could feel it in my belly, my instincts saying we were done here.

Crimson, the beta of the shifters and a powerhouse cougar shifter, was the next to speak. "I can go tonight. I'll take Paul. We can be back by morning with at least twenty miles covered ahead to make sure it is safe for the caravan."

Richard had said nothing since Chris had spoken, listening to us all. At his side, Chris squeezed her hand on his shoulder a little more. He lifted a hand and put it over her fingers. Well shit, this was not going to go well.

I hated when I was right about things like this.

"We stay here, for now," Richard said. "This place is safety, and while we do need to reach the Haven, we don't know how far it is. It could be years away."

"Or weeks," I said. "Or days." I could see the decision had been made, but that didn't mean I was going down without something of a fight. Stupid man, led around by his dick. Suddenly I understood Pam's nickname for him and my frustration flew out of my mouth. "Damn it, Dick, you're going to let her tell you what to do when she has no idea what it is to keep all these people safe? Her fear is going to get people killed. Can you really live with that?"

Chris's eyes flashed and then filled with tears. She turned and ran from the fire. Well, fuck, that went sideways fast. I felt like I was dealing with Jasmine again, lashing out and hurting even when I didn't really mean to.

Richard's mouth dipped downward. "You are not

Pamela, and you are barely part of this caravan, wolf. Remember that. You can be removed."

My eyebrows shot up along with the urge to grab Marley and cut ties with Dick and his group.

But Crimson drew close and put a hand on my arm, stopping me, even as Richard stood and went after his woman. I moved to put a few more inches of space between Crimson and me, but she didn't seem to notice. "He's barely gotten Chris back, and now is afraid to lose her and their child. I believe you are right, Alex. We need to move. We can all smell the rain coming, more with each passing minute."

I glanced at her. "So he'll do as she wants, even if it costs the caravan lives? Is that really what's happening here?"

She drew a breath and then shrugged. "Pamela was the only one that could make him move. She was the caravan witch, and he respected that more than he respected anyone else."

I ran a hand through my hair, thinking, allowing my mind to get worked up over this problem instead of thinking about Pamela and what she was doing right then. Where she was. If she was hurt. If she needed me. I pushed Pam away, tucked her deep into the recesses of my heart.

"Crimson, take Paul and get the lay of the land to the east. I'll see if I can come up with a reason to make them move," I said. She slapped a hand on my back, a searing heat of her life's energy calling to me in that split second before she stepped away and shifted to her four-legged form. As a cougar, she shot forward, a blur of tawny fur against the darkening black of the night. There was a whoosh of wings and then Paul was following her to the far end of the ravine.

Wade folded his arms as he stared out, watching them go too. "Richard is going to be angry with you for going behind his back and sending them out. Leaders like him always get pissy when they are subverted, even if it's for the betterment of the group."

I shrugged. "Whatever. He's blind right now. And he isn't in charge of the shifters."

Not that I was . . . but I was an Alpha and Crimson was responding to me as if I were in charge. I'd take it—for now—and use it to try to help this damn caravan.

"Dick isn't blind, he's avoiding a conflict," Wade said. "There is a difference. The only reason Chris let him back into her bed is because Pamela is gone. Pamela made Richard a better man. Made him stronger, and Chris wants someone she can boss. She can boss him with Pam gone."

"Pamela does that for a lot of us," I said softly.

Wade grunted. "She'd better if what the elementals thinks she is supposed to do is true."

I did a slow turn toward him. "What are you talking about?"

Wade didn't look at me, just kept staring to the east. "The seers of the supernatural world weren't the only ones to write prophecies. The elementals did too. And Pamela and her bloodline is smack dab in the middle of one that has the power to change the world one more time. The power to make it better, or to darken it for an unknowable amount of time."

I closed my eyes, fatigue rolling through me. "How am I not surprised?"

Wade laughed. "From what I've seen so far of young Pam, you shouldn't be."

No, I shouldn't be. But I was—I'd thought that being away from Rylee and her bloodline would be enough to keep us away from prophecies. "Tell me about this prophecy. I hate being blindsided."

He did look at me then. "You sure? Because it is not pretty, there is no good ending that I see for her. And her leaving the caravan with Raven . . . it's the start of the darker path."

"Then all the better that we should be ready for what is coming," I said. Because I'd be damned if I was going to let Pamela go into some wicked prophecy blind, and without me at her side. So the best thing I could do was be as prepared as possible.

But as Wade spoke, my stomach twisted into knots and I fought not to throw up the contents of my belly. Because bad didn't even begin to cover what was about to come our way.

Not even by a little bit.

3

PAMELA

Raven jumped us through the Veil as if it were nothing, no effort, no fatigue. He wove the element of spirit with an ease that made my fumbling with it seem sloppy and inexperienced. Strange, it had always been easy for me to use my elemental powers, but now that they were back and open to me, I felt like I'd never used them before.

Perhaps my years away from my own abilities had reduced my confidence in using them. I blinked, the world bent and twisted, and then we were no longer standing in the ravine far to the north but a place where the heat dropped onto me like a sopping wet, hot wool blanket.

"Oh, that's horrid," Oka muttered. "This is not pleasant at all. What is this place? It feels like I'm walking through a pot of soup."

Her description was perfect, and my lips quirked upward. "A pot of soup indeed."

"This place was once the swamps of the south," Raven

said. "They were broken up into little islands that are spread out over a new ocean, but the heat and humidity didn't change much."

We stood in water up to my knees and Oka lifted a paw. Her fur where it had been in the water was no longer a lovely peach tone, but a muddy brown that stunk vaguely of rotting vegetation. She curled up her nose. "You have a reason for bringing us here?"

Raven nodded, turned and walked away. "Come this way. We need to discuss our plan of attack where we will not be overheard."

Plan of attack. "I thought we were going to rescue Frost?" I stumbled after him, the water and muck underneath pulling at my boots, slowing me down.

"That is what we are doing, but it will take more than just a rescue." Raven didn't look back, but his voice echoed around us. The trees were hung low with moss and lichens that moved in a dull breeze. There were no ripples in the water that I could see. For some reason, I was thinking of oversized crocodiles with strangely painted faces. It took me a moment to realize that I was picking up on Oka's recent memories when we'd been apart.

"You faced a croc that could run on land like a damn horse?" I blurted the question. She bobbed her head.

"That was bad. Jasmine got bit and I had to drag her along. Alex distracted them long enough that we thought we'd escaped." She shook her head and again her memories slid across to me. Seeing Alex chased up the steep slope of a ravine, of Oka biting down on the croc's mouth as she worked with him to save the three of them. How Jasmine had done nothing.

Another flicker of Jasmine in Alex's arms, of them kissing, drew a gasp from me. Oka shook her head. "It's not what you think."

"It doesn't matter what I think," I said softly. "He was never really mine. I . . . was . . . with Mac. I'd let Alex go." Was, past tense. Mac was gone. Pain throbbed anew in my heart, and that tightened my throat and made my eyes well with tears. I dashed them away before they could blind me.

Oka sighed. "I'll tell you what really happened with them, when you're ready. If you want."

We were silent after that. The only sound was our feet plopping in and out of the water as we sloshed along. Raven didn't slow and he didn't look back. He kept moving forward, pushing deeper and deeper into the swamp.

I found myself thinking of Mac more and more. Of what he'd think about this place. Of what he'd say. More than that, I thought about when Faris had first told me he'd send me help. *Beware the bear's bite.* Why had he said that? Mac had been everything I'd needed, everything I'd never known I wanted in a friend, a lover. I shook my head. Faris was likely just being Faris, a.k.a., an ass.

An hour ticked by with my thoughts whirling around themselves, and then almost another before Raven stopped and waited for me to catch up.

"Here." He held his hand out to me and pulled me onto a log that protruded out of the water. I wobbled a minute and then gasped at what I was seeing on the other side.

The nearly pitch-black swamp was gone, and the ground ahead of us was firm, covered in lush green grass and a bloom of flowers that scented the air so heavily with their perfume, I couldn't believe I hadn't been able to smell it before.

A fountain in the center of the glade bubbled up with crystal clear water that caught the light of the moon through a break in the trees and reflected tiny rainbows dancing across the grass. Drinking from the water was a pair of unicorns. They lifted their heads and I was sure that one of them nodded at me, tipping her horn in my direction.

"What is this place?"

"My home . . . for now. The elementals can't find it, so we are safe here. I try to bring a few supernatural creatures to this place when I can, to keep them safe too." He stepped across the log. And I moved to follow.

A thrum of energy cut through the ground under my feet and I swayed where I was, both repulsed and seduced by what rolled through me, from the soles of my feet all the way up to the crown of my head. I stood there and breathed through it, feeling it, tasting it, and half wishing I could keep it for myself.

That is dark power, Pamela, Sam's voice whispered, quieter than before. *Be careful.*

Yeah, I'd picked up on that too. The light didn't tend to seduce you where you stood.

"What is it, though?"

The First Witch is still buried, right?

I bent and put my hand to the earth. I wasn't sure whether I could feel the oubliette I'd stuffed the First

Witch in this far away, but it was worth trying. My fingers sunk into the mucky bottom under the water and I sent out a pulse of power woven with the earth toward the First Witch's cell. A few tense moments passed before I got a ping off the oubliette.

"No, it's still there." Another rush of power worked its way up my legs, pooling in my belly, warmth spreading in a direction that I had to fight to breathe through. The world narrowed to a pinprick of light and I clung to it as I worked to shake the sensations.

Then perhaps she has someone looking for her. That would not bode well for her to be on this side of the Veil and set free from the oubliette.

Sweet goddess of the earth, it would *not* be good. Oka watched me, her eyes narrowed. "I do not like that you talk to it."

It, being Sam.

I reached for her. "I know." There was nothing else I could say, nothing that would convince her that Sam was not going to hurt me, that ultimately Sam's purpose was to keep me alive. Hell, I didn't even think that I fully trusted my dark magic, but I understood her better now.

Across the log, Raven waited for me. His eyes were sharp and full of questions, but he asked me nothing.

I stood and walked across the line between the swamp and the clearing, Oka close behind. She didn't shift to her smaller form as we walked across the thick grass. If anything, her fur stood up along her spine as we walked. "This place is too good to be true."

"It feels like an elemental home," I said softly. "Like

before the world broke and they were separate from the rest of us."

"Because that's exactly what this is," Raven said. He swept off his cloak and sat on the edge of the fountain. The two unicorns touched their noses to his hand and then wandered toward the flowering willow trees at the end of the clearing. "It takes an incredible amount of spirit to create a place like this, which is why it is not very big. It was all I could do." He spread his fingers over the water and a thin spout rose, and he drank from it.

"Show-off," Oka muttered.

I smiled, but it was a tired smile. I was, to say the least, exhausted, and I knew we were only just starting this journey.

"We will rest here for the remainder of the night," Raven said.

"We need to get to Frost," I said, panic hitting me suddenly, a blow of anxiety I didn't understand slamming into me. "I thought that was what we were doing? We should go now. He needs us!"

"I do not know where he is. You are still recovering from the effects of what you have accomplished with healing the Veil, and he is technically safe. The elementals will not harm him." Raven looked away from me with that last line and I knew he was not telling me the whole truth, or at least that he wasn't sure. No surprise there.

"A few hours then. And I assume you have something of a plan?" I prodded, trying to get him to give me something to ease my mind. My heart was pounding and that same urge to move my feet climbed over me.

"I am not my younger sister." He smiled. "Of course I have a plan." Raven finally looked at me and shook his head. "How are you still clean after walking through that swamp?"

I looked down at my clothes. They were what I'd been given within the Veil as protection. Pants, corset and shirt, and solid black boots, leather and some lace—not a flick of mud had stuck to them. They looked as though they were cleanly pressed only moments before.

Magic clothes indeed. I should have had these years ago.

"Lucky, I guess." I wanted to look at him, ask him all the questions I had bubbling up in my mind about my mother, my magic, about Frost and how we were going to find him, but I refrained. Mostly because I was tired, and with each moment that passed, that fatigue crawled over me more. The grass was soft, and Oka was already lying down. I went to my knees and curled up with her the way we had done for years as we'd survived with only each other to depend on.

The ground seemed to draw me down and gave way under me like a mattress, drawing me into the warmth, and I couldn't help the sigh that slid out of my lips. The light around us darkened—and while I suspected it was Raven "turning out the lights"—I just didn't care. I closed my eyes and fell asleep, knowing I was safe, knowing that at least for a few hours I could rest.

Yes, I know what you're thinking, how could that be? It couldn't be, that was just it.

My sleep dragged me down deep, so deep that I could actually feel my heartbeat slow.

I wanted so badly to rest, to not have any dreams or nightmares. But it was not to be, not for me.

I opened my eyes and I was lying with Oka still, but I knew I was asleep. That same curl of seductive power wrapped around me and tugged me forward. Maybe I should have pushed it away, but there was something I needed in it. Strength. Power. The ability to protect those I loved.

That power hummed through me and I held it tightly. This was the darker side of my magic—I knew that, but I also knew I needed it as surely as I needed any other of my powers.

I pushed to my feet as a voice from my past called to me. One I knew better than I knew maybe any other. A scream from her throat was like a knife to my heart.

No, not her. Don't hurt her.

"Rylee!" I screamed back, just her name, as I bolted. I hate to say it, but I stumbled I was running so fast, right back into the swamp. Through the thick water, I pulled myself along, not caring that I was being slapped with branches and twigs, that I was being sucked into the mud deeper and deeper. Only that I heard her voice and she was pissed off and yelling at the top of her lungs.

Anger and fear, I heard them both in her voice. This was not good, not good at all.

I tumbled over an unseen log and went into the water, over my head, and came up spluttering. The scene had changed and there she was, right in front of me. Not in the swamp, but in what looked like the farmyard of her place in North Dakota, though the buildings were different. They were a mimic of the past.

I don't know how I was seeing this place, but I was certain this was really happening. This was no dream. I was seeing the truth.

Truth. This is the truth.

Three people stood in front of her, and I knew in a split second that they were elementals from their clothing to the weapons they held, and their condescending looks.

They were not the good kind of elementals. Strange that I could make that judgment so quickly, but there it was, and I knew it was *truth* in the center of my being. They were stiff and leaned toward her, trying to force her to do something. Trying to intimidate her, which I knew wouldn't go well for them.

"You can fuck right off on the horse you fucking well rode in on." Rylee barked the words, her red hair swirling up in a gust of wind. "This is my land."

"You are a daywalking vampire, and can claim no land as your own. You are to be a subject to my queen," the only male elemental said, his voice snobby and full of derision. His white hair and clothing marked him as a sylph.

Of the other two, one was a sylph, marked as well with the same hair, and one a female undine, a water elemental with dark blue hair and pale, pale skin.

Rylee's hand went to one of the swords she carried on her back. "You sure you want to make the mistake and cross that line? Because you can die, just like any other fucking trespasser. Makes no damn difference to me." She pointed at the ground between them with her free hand.

The three elementals stared at her, the tension rising

in the air, and then they stepped away from the literal line in the sand.

"We will be back," the male sylph said. "Three days. You will either bow to our queen, or we will destroy you and all you hold dear. Including your brats. Including your harpy. Your man. Everything."

Rylee's body language shifted, and I knew what was coming. "I don't do well with threats, fucker. So let me be clear. I will bow to no one, and I'm done with you and your bullshit. You come back, and I'm going to assume you want a fucking war." She snarled and the sword came clear of its sheath with a slick move that was so fast my eyes couldn't follow the blade. Apparently the sylph couldn't either because he just stood there as his arm fell to the ground where she'd cut it off.

He stood for a second before the blood began to pour and his friends grabbed him and scrambled away, the second sylph lifting the three of them up and away from Rylee. "You'll pay for this!" the wounded sylph screamed.

I moved forward, trying to get close to her. "Rylee, I'm here!" I choked on the words.

She turned, ever so slightly, her head cocked. Her eyes were different now, no longer the eyes of a Tracker, but still they were all Rylee. "Pam?"

Goddess, she'd heard me! "I'm coming, Rylee. I won't let them hurt you and the babies! I won't. I'll do whatever I have to!" I was sobbing the words, in part from seeing her, in part from realizing how much danger they were in. She could not face elementals on her own. She was no magic user.

Truth.

33

She drove her sword into the ground and closed her eyes. "Pam? If you can hear me . . . come home. It's time. You've been away too long . . . and we need you now more than ever. Come home."

Sobs ripped out of my chest so hard and deep that I woke myself in the clearing. Oka was awake next to me, her head butting up against mine. "What happened? You were crying out in your sleep."

"My family is in trouble, Oka." I wrapped my arms around her. "We have to hurry and find Frost. I have to get back to Rylee before the elementals kill her."

Because there was no way Rylee would bow to anyone, not even for her life.

4

─────────

I tried to go back to sleep, the mossy warm ground, hidden and safe in the sanctuary that Raven had brought us to, and the low rumble of Oka soothing me should have done just that. The best I could manage was a fitful doze that dragged me in and out of old nightmares, of seeing Rylee, Liam, and my family killed by elementals, of watching Mac die in my arms, of all I loved being stripped away from me, of taking strength in the darkest parts of my soul, of using all I had at my disposal and not caring—I think that might have been the worst.

To see that perhaps the darkness in me was what I needed more than the light. What would I give to save those I loved? Everything. I would give everything.

I finally woke as the light changed in Raven's special clearing, my cheeks stiff with dried tears.

"That was not restful for you. You look like you've been pulled through a knot hole backwards," Oka said, her usual blunt self. I sat up and rubbed at my face, working away the salt stains.

"Better than nothing at all, I guess." That's what I told myself as I pushed slowly to my feet, my body aching as though I'd been beaten repeatedly. Raven leaned against the fountain, his head tipped back and eyes closed. He looked younger there with his body in sleep and his face not closed off from giving too much away. Nor did he look to be having any more of a restful sleep than I had.

"No, don't take her. Don't take her from me," he mumbled and lifted a hand as though to grab hold of something. I couldn't help it, I reached out and caught his hand with my own.

His fingers tightened and he pulled me closer. I went to my knees and he opened his eyes. Fear and sadness ruled there in the blue depths and that bothered me more than when I wasn't sure what he was thinking. "The elementals are hunting you, Pamela. They can't find you right now because you are here, but the second you step out of this clearing we will have a limited time before they catch up to us."

I didn't let his hand go, nor did he try to pull away from me. "How long do you think it will take to find Frost?" I found myself not wanting to tell him about the danger Rylee was in. He wouldn't understand how much she meant to me, that Rylee was like a mixture of mother and sister. That I needed to save her as much as I needed to save Frost.

He shrugged. "Hours if we're lucky. It will depend on just how they are tracking you."

I didn't like the sound of that. "You mean like a Tracker?"

"None left, none but Marcella, Rylee's daughter," he

said softly, "and she is far too young. Plus, they don't know that she will be a Tracker for years yet, not until she is grown."

Marcella was Rylee and Liam's daughter. I stared at him. "So how can they find us?"

"Find you," he corrected. It was only then I realized that the bands that had held some of his elements away from him were missing.

I touched his wrists. "How did you get them off?"

"A very old friend finally saw that I was not done with meddling in this world, that my strengths could still help." He smiled but it slid from his face quickly. "I was coming to take your bands off when you stumbled out of the Veil."

I'd wondered how he'd appeared so quickly, but with all that had been going on, it had been the least of my concerns. "Back to the first question, how are they tracking me?"

"You are not the only witch; you are not the only half-breed. Which means there are others out there—perhaps not as strong as you—that have a skill set of both witch and elemental, which means they have the ability to use tracking spells and the power to do it. Any point along the way if they managed to get some of your blood, they can use that to trace you anywhere."

I closed my eyes, thinking back to all the fights, all the wounds, all the blood I'd spilled over the last three years. There could have been any number of times that it was taken and protected to be used. "That's how they knew to come after the caravan. Because I had been there."

At his quizzical look, I explained about facing each of the elementals in order to get my bands removed, but also how I'd faced them in dreamscapes. And how one of those dreamscapes had been at the caravan.

"It's possible there is a lag time of sorts between where you are and when they get the information." Raven nodded. "That could help us."

Oka padded over and sat next to me. "Or it could be that they made an assumption as to where she was going to be. She's been with the caravan for months now."

"That too. Either way, we have to treat each moment out of a sanctuary like this with trepidation." He paused. "There is no way we can know when they will be on us, and how many of them."

"Like a swarm of bees," I said.

"Worse," Oka grumbled. "Wasps. Wasps are assholes."

I put an arm around her. "You are not wrong, my friend."

Raven stood and I followed. "We'll step out and jump the Veil to where my sister has many of the terralings hidden away. That is the best place to start. It is farther north and to the east than the original home of the—"

"I can just jump us to Frost," I said. Jumping to a person's location was an ability I had, that even Raven hadn't been able to duplicate, and it would shorten this trip tremendously. Not that it dealt with the issue of the elementals, but at least my baby brother would be safe. And that was what really mattered here. Because the faster we got him clear of the elementals, the faster I could go to Rylee. The faster I could go home. Three days. I had three days to get Frost and then to Rylee.

I stepped out of the clearing as Raven grabbed for my cloak. "No, Pamela, don't do that!"

"It's fine. I know it's been a while but I'm sure I can still do it." Hell, I'd jumped to a person instead of a place without knowing what I was doing when he'd first taught me how to jump the Veil. Oka shifted to her house cat form and leapt to my shoulder as Raven grabbed at me again.

"No, Pamela, listen to me! This is not the way, it's dangerous—"

Only I didn't listen. I wove spirit through me and Oka and thought about Frost, thought about finding him and seeing his little face and bright blue eyes again. Raven let me go a split second before I finished the weave, in time to hear him yell.

"It won't work when the person you seek is hidden!"

Hidden? That made no sense, at least not at first. The world around me warped and danced, but I didn't pop out somewhere else. I didn't find myself *anywhere*. The place I was didn't feel like it was solid, or even real with the way the light cut through mist that spilled out all around me, as though I were floating in clouds that were not clouds.

The space around me spun and I stared at a single point as I tried to orient myself. "Oka, where are we?"

"I don't know, but I think I'm going to be sick. We need to stop spinning right now." She gagged as if to impress on me the urgency of standing still.

I widened my stance and made myself stare into the distance. I tried weaving spirit to take me back to Raven, but the weave did nothing. Not that spirit wasn't there, but it was like I was . . . stuck in between? That wasn't quite right. No, it was like being inside one of the elemental's havens. Like being inside Raven's home.

Inside those places, you couldn't use spirit. A throw-back rule to the days when spirit users were plentiful and dangerous at the very least. I lifted a hand and reached through the mist. The air swirled ahead of me, and there was a moment where I thought I could see a figure in the distance.

Damn it, I have no ability with this jumping around nonsense, Sam said softly. Distantly as if she too were fading.

From my shoulder, Oka gagged and then pressed her face against my neck. "Tell me when the ride is over."

My stomach didn't roll, or at least not for the same reason hers twisted. "Oka, I think we are stuck some-where we shouldn't be."

"And where would that be?" she mumbled. "The Veil?"

I thought about that possibility and dismissed it. "I don't think so."

Not the Veil, but not the real world either.

Where in the hell were we?

5

ALEX

W ade's voice was a careful monotone, as if by keeping his words without inflection they would not seem so bad. But even there, with the caravan close by, and no immediate danger, I'd never thought the world looked so dark. Especially for me, especially for Pam.

"The prophecy is an old one, and it is specific to a bloodline like Pamela's. A few of the elementals who were aware of it saw her as a child and believed her to be the one it referred to." He paused and then bobbed his head as if encouraging himself. "When the world has been broken beyond repair and the threads that tie the elements together sheared, then shall the witch of magic and elemental blood come forward. Her life will matter not, but her deeds will be that which will either save or destroy what is left of the world. To destroy, she must turn away from the darkness. To save, she must go into the final embrace of the darkness, taking it into herself.

Only by balancing the light and the dark can the world finally come to a place of harmony."

"Holy shit, there is no winning for her—" I said, and he cut me off.

"To find that balance, she must take on the crown of darkness," Wade said, then stopped and frowned. "Do you understand what that means?"

I frowned back at him, and then shook my head. Something about crown of darkness niggled at me, but I couldn't put my finger on it. Around us a few splats of rain hit the ground. "No, I don't—"

"The elementals have their suspicions," he said.

"How do you even know this? You left them, and were hiding with Stefan and his Breakers?"

Wade flushed. "I . . . listened in to Raven speaking to himself while Pamela was out. He didn't know I was there, and he kept repeating the prophecy over and over. As if he were trying to figure it out."

He might as well have punched me in the gut the way I lost my wind on that bit of information. "Are you serious? Raven knows about this prophecy?"

Wade nodded. "He was worried, that much was obvious. I mean, he didn't even notice that I was close by, and for a man of his abilities, that surprised me."

Raven had taken Pam away . . . but was there more to it than finding Frost? Was he going to try to force her down one of those paths? And if so, which one?

The rain picked up, big fat drops hitting the top of my head, soaking me in seconds. I put my hands on my hips, and looked into the storm-covered sky, letting the rain wash over me, wash the dust of the day away. I lowered my face to look back at the elemental. "This is bad, Wade."

"I know. I don't think anything can be done, but you love her. I figured you should know."

I loved Pam, that was true. "For now, we just—"

"Incoming!" A shout cut through the air. I spun to see a bear shifter running full tilt toward the caravan. The rain suddenly came down so hard, it was difficult to see his dark figure, just a shadow of movement was all I caught.

"Incoming what?" I yelled as I bolted in the direction that the bear shifter had come from, my body zinging with adrenaline as I raced toward whatever danger had arrived with the storm. Above my head, a flash of lightning arced across the sky quickly followed by a booming rumble of thunder that shook the ground with intensity. Another wave of rain fell in sheets, slashing against my bare arms and face like tiny needles. Something about the sudden ferocity of the storm had me pausing. "Wade, is this elementals?"

"I don't know." He slid to a stop beside me and pointed to the far end of the ravine. "Doesn't matter, this is bad!" I could barely hear him over the pounding rain. I'd never seen droplets so fat, they were the size of tennis balls. Each one hit and drenched you, as if on their own they'd drown you.

Wade pointed again at the far end of the ravine. Over the pounding of water, the boom of thunder, there was something new. An undertone that made my blood cool. The sound of rushing water, and with the next flash of lightning we could see clearly what was coming our way.

"Flash flood!" I yelled, trying to be heard over the storm.

Damn it, I hated being right, but I'd thought we'd have more time. Then again, I'd never seen rain like this before.

"Everybody, up, let's go!" I roared the words as the sound of a distant engine reached my ears. Only it wasn't an engine, but the thundering of water as it rushed down the narrow gulches to the west of us, overwhelming the banks of the river as it went.

I ran back through the caravan, yelling, waking people up, shaking tents. "Move, move! Flash flood!"

The caravan lurched into action and people pulling their shit together faster than I'd thought. Then again, this would not be the first time they'd had to run from danger in the middle of the night.

The rain was not helping as it soaked everything and everyone, but they didn't slow and neither did I.

I pulled tents apart with the rest of them, scrambling to salvage what we could in the few minutes we had before the water hit us full on. "Someone get me an ETA on that water!" I yelled.

One of the shifters bolted off, badger by the striped hair. But I had no time to make more than a nod in his direction. The two trucks started up and I threw people and gear into them as fast as I could. As soon as the first was full, I sent it off. "Go, go!"

Richard found me, hair plastered to his head as I prepped the second truck. "Are you sure?" he asked, his eyes still blurred with sleep.

"He's just doing this to make his point," Chris snapped,

as soaked as he was. Were they that fucking stupid? Gods, no wonder they drove Pam batty.

Another time I would have snapped right back at her, matching her tone, but I didn't need to as the stream we had been set up next to swelled its banks suddenly, and without warning, washing up over our feet and rising above our ankles in seconds.

"Go!" I threw a few more pots and an older woman into the back of the truck. I wasn't being terribly careful, but the time for careful was over and done. We needed to move, and move now.

The second truck started forward, heading toward the eastern side of the ravine. There was a track big enough for the vehicles if they went one at a time. The real question was would they make it before the water hit their back tires? Even as it was, the hill was going to be a bitch, sloppy with the hard rain, and slick like ogre snot.

I turned to see what was left of the camp, just as a wave of water peeked over the top edge of the ravine. The western side of the ravine had a waterfall that turned into the stream that ran through the middle. The ravine itself was not massive in width, more in length.

The wave that swelled above the ravine at the precipice of the waterfall was nothing short of massive. A hundred feet high if I were to guess. And it shot out in a burst, like a ball out of a cannon. The water was a dark spew in the night and it fell crashing to the stream below. With that fall of water, the skies darkened further with a single gust of wind, bringing even more clouds in and opening them up like a zipper, as if the rain that had been falling before hadn't been enough.

"Fuck, I should have pushed Dick to move sooner." I spun and ran toward the eastern side of the ravine. The first truck was almost to the top of the edge, and it held much of the food and supplies. But the second truck full of people had been caught in the rain and the instant mud created in the loose soil.

"Push it!" I yelled as I got closer. A few of the men jumped out and tried to push it, but the truck was sliding. I didn't slow as I reached the truck, bent my shoulder and jammed it against the metal tailgate, pushing for all I was worth. The deep growl of the river getting closer drove me more than anything else. I found myself looking up into the faces of the remaining kids, the ones that Pamela had fought to protect over anyone or anything else.

"You can do it," a little girl, Ruby, whispered, as she reached out and patted me on the head. A tiny spurt of energy slid from her into me—not anything I'd taken, but an offering.

As if she knew exactly what she was doing, as if she knew that her life depended on this moment.

I bent into the truck, braced my feet and snarled as I shoved the truck. Behind us, the water slammed into the edge of the track, eroding what the truck sat on.

"Ropes, get ropes on the front!" I didn't slow my own pushing to help them; we had to steady the truck on one end, and pull it on the other. Shouting and hollering commenced, but I heard none of it as the truck began to slide backward in the mud, the tires spinning but getting no traction, the rain coming down, the water rising faster than a sinking ship went under the waves.

If there was a time when Pamela and her magic could

be useful, this was it. What I wouldn't give for a little elemental help . . . shit. "Wade! Come on, man!"

"I'm trying!" He was somewhere to my right and I couldn't see him. "This storm is not natural, several elementals are working together to make it happen, I think." In other words, his own abilities didn't come up to snuff.

"Well, keep trying!" I assumed he was an elemental who had connection to the earth, but if that was so, he was doing a piss-poor job of shoring things up. "The sides of the track, can you firm that up?"

"Oh."

Jesus balancing on a tin can in a dark alley, had he really not thought of that? I turned my head to glare at him through the torrential rain, even as the ground below us firmed up a little, the water sloughing off. The truck lurched forward a few feet and then we were at the top of the ravine. Barely.

The truck stopped and I smacked the side of it as I walked up. "Keep going."

"That's not your call." Dick walked toward me from the other direction, his face streaked with mud, rain, and indignation.

I got right in his space, stared him down and let both the Alpha and the incubus in me come fully to the surface, let him see just what he was dealing with—I was done playing nice if he wasn't done playing stupid. "Your call to stay about got the entire caravan nearly wiped out. We keep moving. Wade says there are elementals behind this, which means they want what you've got."

Dick paled visibly even in the dark and cleared his

throat. "Keep moving . . . right. Then . . . we'll go till dawn?"

I nodded. That would be good enough for now.

The trucks rolled forward and most of the shifters climbed into the back of the bigger truck, the one Oka and I had brought back from the Breakers along with their stash of food and supplies. I drew a breath and gave a full-body shiver that I couldn't stop. Only then did my muscles remind me that pushing a truck uphill in the rain was a rather difficult thing to do. With aching legs, I let myself fall back, following the trucks slowly, letting them pull away as I caught my breath.

Wade dropped back with me, his eyes downcast. "I'm sorry about back there."

"You caught us at the end, so don't apologize. But I don't understand just what you *were* doing?" If anything. Those two unspoken words hung between us.

The rain continued to hammer down around us, the ground softening with each step we took. "I'm not very strong, Alex," Wade said. "My connection to the earth is all I have, but I was barely above a field planter in the scheme of my world."

I racked my brain to try to understand what he meant. He must have seen my struggle because he quickly explained.

"Basically, I can call seedlings to life, and I can do a little work with the earth, but nothing like many of those who are terralings. I'm just not very strong." He shrugged. "And I didn't think about the truck. I was just trying to stop the water, but of course that was futile as a bumblebee in a windstorm."

A hard gust of wind snapped against our backs, pushing us forward. No rain though. I looked over my shoulder to see the flashing white of a figure swooping out of the sky above us. I pushed Wade to the side and jumped in the other direction just before the figure cut between us, landing lightly on her feet.

She turned, her white clothes pristine, her nearly silver white hair flowing around her as though the rain didn't bother her. And maybe it didn't.

I was pretty sure she was a sylph. Her eyes narrowed as they landed on Wade. "Dirty, weak terraling, where is the witch? If you are keeping her hidden, we will find her. She has to die."

Pam, she meant Pam. I didn't even think if what I was doing was a bad idea or not, I just reacted. With a snarl, I jumped toward her, catching her by surprise as I tackled her to the muddy ground. She let out a grunt as we hit hard, me on top of her. Maybe I should have felt bad about tackling a woman without first asking her just what she thought she was doing. But I'd seen the power of elementals at their worst and I wasn't about to give her a chance. And she wanted to kill Pam.

I grabbed her around the throat with both hands and held her in the mud. "You're going to talk or I'm going to snap your neck like a barnyard chicken."

Her eyes widened and under my hand her throat worked to swallow, bobbing against my skin.

"I am the queen's consort and I will not be spoken to—"

I squeezed until her eyes bugged out and then eased

off. The wind around us picked up and I braced my body for the impact.

When it hit, it lifted us both off the ground. But I wasn't about to let her go. Not now.

I had a damn tiger by the tail and letting go would only get me bitten.

Damn it, where was Oka when the jokes were about tigers?

"Kill her!" Wade yelled from below. I didn't think he was wrong, but I wanted to know if the prophecy he'd told me was true, or just something he'd heard, and the only way to find out was from another elemental.

"Why do you want to kill Pam?" I snarled the words and flexed my muscles, drawing the sylph close enough that we were nose to nose and she was staring into my eyes. The incubus in me woke up, whispering to her through the skin-to-skin contact. The wind slowed and we lowered to the ground as the heat between us spiked and she moaned, her eyelashes fluttering.

My incubus powers surged and I gritted my teeth, fighting them, to keep them in check for a few moments. I couldn't let her go. And I couldn't let my power have her.

"Tell me why you want her dead," I repeated.

"She is the one of the prophecy. There is no way for her but through the darkness unless we kill her. If we kill her, the world will be safer. We believe that." Her words chilled me more than when her hands swept up to the sides of my face, cupping my head and drawing me down as if to kiss me. I jerked my face to the side and she let her fingers trail down my neck to my shoulders. "If I tell you everything, you'll kiss me?"

"Yes." I didn't even hesitate. I couldn't help the desire that poured off my skin, and made me want to fuck her over in more ways than one. But I didn't think it was a true desire for her body, but for what it encapsulated— her life. I wanted her life, no different than a damn vampire. I fought the urge to just drink her down as the wind eased around us.

"Hurry, whatever you're going to do, hurry," Wade said. "There are two other elementals coming and we must be free of them."

I stared into the sylph's eyes. "Tell me everything you can."

"She is of the bloodline that will be the end of all the endings. She is the witch that we wanted dead because with her gone, she could not embrace the darkness. As hard to kill as she has proven, we will come for her. We must, we must stop her from taking the crown of darkness."

Damn it, Wade was right about that part then.

"Who is 'we'? And what is the crown of darkness?"

Her eyelids fluttered. "All of us. It is all of us. The crown . . . the heir to the first darkness, she will place it on her head."

"Hurry, Alex!" Wade shouted. I turned, the sylph still in my hands, still fluttering her eyelashes up at me.

Two elementals strode toward us, one of them a lithe woman with blue-green hair and clothes that moved as though they floated in water, and the other a man dressed all in browns so that he blended in with the earth. I stared at them as I held their friend tightly by the throat. "I suggest you look elsewhere for her. Pam isn't here."

They laughed, and then they stopped as I held the sylph up higher with one hand. She didn't struggle against my hold even as I tightened my fingers. She moaned and arched her back and began to pull off her clothes. Her hands slid down her bare skin as I choked her.

"What are you doing to her?" The blue-green-haired woman's horror was more than apparent. I stared right back at her, wondering if I could reach her from this far away with my incubus abilities.

"She attacked us, as did you. Should there not be a consequence?" I winked at the blue-green-haired woman, sending out a tendril of my power to her, feeling it wrap around her body, sliding under her clothes and tugging at her desires. She wobbled where she stood and then let out a low moan, matching the sylph's as her hands went to her clothes.

"Goddess, yes, don't stop," she whimpered.

"What the fuck is going on?" The man—who I could only assume was an earth elemental—flipped his hand toward me. The earth bucked up under my feet, but I didn't drop the sylph. I drew her to me and kissed her hard, sucking her life down in big gulps that made the incubus in my unequivocally pleased. More than that, her energy was so much stronger than that of Jasmine's, deeper and full of notes and flavors that were there and gone in flashes that made my mouth ache to take it all in. I wanted all of her, to drink her down until there was nothing left, like a perfect meal.

Her life force was close to the end when I pulled back from her and dropped her to the ground. There was no true understanding of what I was doing, as I was just following the instincts and urges rolling through me now. I spun and pointed a finger at the second woman and she flipped onto her back, arching her body as though I were touching her.

"Take them, and do not bother the caravan again or I will kill them both," I said. My voice had deepened and was thick and sluggish as though I'd indeed just been disturbed by him while fucking the two women. Even then, as full as I was, the life force of the blue-green-haired woman called to me and I wanted to feel her mouth on mine. To taste her and see if she was salty like the ocean.

I gritted my teeth and struggled to keep the emotions, and the giant damn erection that was currently trying to get my attention, in check.

The man all dressed in brown grabbed at the woman on the ground. As soon as he touched her, his eyes rolled and he sunk to his knees.

"He's not going to . . ." Wade trailed off as the earth elemental stripped his clothes and the woman next to him did the same.

"Yeah, he's going to." I backed away from the sylph, turned and shifted into my wolf form. That helped with everything going through my body, the energy and the urge to grab hold of that strange elemental and—no, I had to block that from my mind. I was not my father. Maybe I could drink them down, but that didn't mean that I was going to fuck everything before I ate it.

Don't play with your food, Alex. I could almost hear Oka laughing at me.

I bolted along after the caravan, lost in my own head.

The elementals had confirmed what Wade had already told me about Pamela. They wanted her dead, out of the way of whatever prophecy they believed she was part of. A crown of darkness . . . that had me more than a little worried. Pam wasn't any safer now that the First Witch was trapped away, not with the elementals hunting her down.

Ahead of us the tail end of the caravan came into view and the morning light peeked up ahead of us, the mountains in the distance lighting.

The rain eased off, the last of the storm blowing over and away from the caravan now that there were no elementals driving it.

I shifted back to two legs, clothing intact. That was a trick I should have learned a long time ago. Oka had been right about that. I rubbed a hand over my face, lethargy kicking in hard.

"You shouldn't have done that. You shouldn't have fought them like that," Wade said, out of breath but catching up to me. Which was saying something, seeing as I'd been running full tilt on four legs.

"I couldn't let them see us as weak."

"No, not that. You shouldn't have let them live, Alex. Because now they're pissed and you've made them a damn mockery humping in the mud. Elementals are nothing if not prideful, and you've just handed them a whole plate full of humble pie."

Well, shit.

6

PAMELA

Through the fog of the dream world, a figure stepped out, dark hair and golden eyes locking onto me.

"Alex." I whispered his name and everything around me seemed to fade. Even Oka. He strode across the distance between us, intensity and lust rolling off him, dragging me toward him whether I wanted it or not.

Before I could say anything else his hands were on me, and his mouth clamped over mine as if I were air and he was drowning. I kissed him back, hanging onto him, even if I didn't understand how he could be here in this place.

Did I care really? No, I loved him, and maybe that last goodbye wasn't the last after all.

At least that's what I thought.

And then the power of the incubus roared through him and into me. Not just lust, but that energy-sucking power that would kill me if I let it.

Truth.

I pushed away from him. "No. Not until you can

control yourself. You need to be able to control yourself, Alex."

His eyes were fogged with desire and his hair was mussed as if he'd been rolling around on the ground. He seemed to be struggling with something and I thought maybe he was trying to tell me something.

"You can figure this out. You just need to wake up," he said, his voice soft, sultry, tugging on my body as if he knew it inside out. I pressed a hand to my belly and swallowed hard.

"Wake up, as if this is a dream?" I looked to Oka and she nodded.

"I think that's what this is, a place of dreams."

The feel of Alex's hands on my body, the pressure of his fingers digging into my ass, and his mouth on mine lingered long after he'd disappeared into the fog, leaving my skin tingling and my heart racing.

Oka stood next to me in her tiger form. She'd claimed she felt less dizzy than when she sat on my shoulder in her house cat form.

"There's not even a place in the levels of the Veil to account for this," I grumbled as I forced my feet to move, to walk in what I hoped was a straight line. Because if what Alex had said was true, then I just needed to wake up. Of course, I really had no idea how to do that.

"Maybe it's a new place in the Veil?" Oka padded next to me, close enough that with each stride her ribcage bumped into my hip. I dropped a hand to her back, understanding the need to stay in contact with one another. This place was trippy, and the last thing I wanted was to be separated.

A shiver ran down my spine as the not-very-distant memories of working through the First Witch's maze caught hold of me. Of the skin bag monsters, the horde of rats, the trials set ahead to test me, to push me to my limits and then beyond. Those shivers turned into tremors that paired up with a sudden cold sweat as it slid down my spine.

I blinked rapidly as the light around us shifted, dimming to a dull gray. "Oh, this cannot be anything good."

Oka lifted her head and sniffed the air. "I don't smell anything."

"Doesn't mean something isn't going to sneak up and bite us in the ass." Still hanging onto her, I did a half turn. There to our right, another tall figure strode our way, cutting through the mist as though they were a hot blade against butter. Not Alex this time, though. A sword hung at the person's side and they lifted it and pointed at us.

Codswallop.

I tugged on Oka and hurried her forward. "I can't use spirit here, so let's not try to make any new friends."

Oka picked up a jog alongside me and despite the dimming light, we hurried away from the figure.

Only there wasn't just one figure, but another to our left. And then more behind us.

"Dreams," Oka whispered, hunching down. "If these are dreams, then we are seeing people that are dreaming, right? They shouldn't be able to hurt us."

"That would seem logical." I paused, slowing my feet. "Though I'm not sure how logical a place where we are stuck in a dream is."

The figures popped in and out of existence around us; some of them were clearly asleep, their faces ones I didn't recognize, but every part of them was clear as day from the frown lines in their foreheads, to the scars on their skin, to the color of their eyes and hair.

One popped up right beside me and roared in my face. A face I knew, Jimmy, from the caravan. Only Jimmy here was pissed, not the easygoing guy I knew. I snapped a hand up and grabbed hold of him by the arm. His face blanked out, and then slowly faded, disappearing until his eyes were all that were left, glowing in the dark.

That reminded me too much of the maze and the glowing firelight eyes of the trapped souls that followed me around.

"What happened?" Oka asked as I drew my hand back.

"I don't know, but obviously it's not the same as Alex."

Or maybe I just loved Alex enough to not send him into oblivion. I gasped at the thought. Had I just killed Jimmy? No, that was not it. I would know if I killed someone.

Truth.

Thank you, Sam, I thought softly. For helping me know which way was which.

I could almost feel her purr with pleasure at my thanks, and that made me smile.

"What if you took hold of one of them before they woke up?" Oka said. "Alex let go of you and backed away, but what if he'd kept holding your hand? Maybe he could have pulled you through."

Her line of reasoning was about as solid as I could put

together too. "I'm not sure I want to try, after this one disappearing."

"He was being aggressive. Try someone who is not so angry," Oka said. She had a point, and I made myself nod.

Carefully I wove my way between the figures, looking for someone that looked normal. Not dangerous. Not angry. And found myself struggling. So many of those people dreaming were furious, and striking out at me, at others. They'd see me and take a swing with whatever weapon they had in hand, and then they'd disappear.

After the fourth such encounter, I took a few steps back. "This isn't just a dreamscape, Oka. It's like . . . the deepest part of someone's dreams. I can't imagine they are waking up the second they take a swing at us."

"Perhaps there are levels of dreaming, just like levels of the Veil?" she offered. Her words rang a bell inside my head, resonating with a truth I felt even if I didn't fully understand it, the same way Sam's words sometimes did.

"If that's true, then there has to be a way out of here, to the waking world. A doorway, something like the way the Veil used to have doorways into the real world." I did a slow spin and lifted one hand as I called up a breeze that would blow the mists away.

Unlike spirit, my connection to air was stronger, and the mists fluttered for a moment before they began to swirl and push away from me. I expected to see solid footing, perhaps rock or dirt, and a place out in nature, maybe a cave.

That wasn't what I got at all. As the mist cleared, the scene that rose around us shocked me more than I cared to admit. The footing showed itself to be solid stone, yes, but stone cut into perfect rectangles and set into the base of a castle I knew all too well. My heart rate kicked up more than a few notches. Was this real? Or had I somehow created this out of my own memories?

"This place, it's a pivot point for the Veil, or it was," I whispered, almost afraid to speak too loud and somehow break the spell of what I was seeing.

"What do you mean, it was?" Oka pushed me to the side to avoid another figure that reached for us, crying, before she disappeared into another dream.

"This castle was set up in England, and it was a place that sat within the Veil. But not fully in it. Straddling the realms." I pointed at the different parts of the castle. "Each doorway took you to a different part of the real world. Some of them took you deeper into the Veil. Some to the demon world." There had been one door in particular that had caused more grief than I wanted to remember on the top floor, where Liam had died.

I drew a slow breath and pushed away memories of a knife and the blood of one of the people I loved best in the world coating my hands.

I stood there, breathing in the past, feeling that moment as the one that started me on the path I stood on now. Was it his fault I had to struggle this way? Liam's fault that I'd become as hard as I was? That I'd been alone for so long? A slow-burning anger started, one that maybe had always been there. His death had cut me deeper than anyone realized, and that wound hadn't healed as I'd thought.

"Easy, Pamela," Oka said, butting her head against me. "The mist is coming back."

She was right and I swirled a blast of cold air through the castle, driving the mist back farther. I didn't understand how this place could be when I'd seen it burn to the ground. The answer was there, right at the edge of my mind, but I wasn't sure that it mattered at the moment. Maybe I'd find out later. Or maybe this really was something from my own mind, some way to deal with an escape from this place.

I took a few steps, gained my bearings and then headed right into the castle. The heels of my boots clattered on the stone as I strode through the doors of the castle. So many battles had been here, so many fights to keep the world free of darkness. I shook my head and turned away from the main courtyard and all the memories it stirred. I headed for the large wooden door that led down into the belly of the castle. "If this is somehow a mirror image of the original castle . . ." I pushed the door open and held it for Oka. She stepped through and I lifted a hand, lighting a flame in my open palm. The flickering light illuminated the narrow, cold, stone-lined hallway that dropped off precariously down a flight of stairs with no railing, and seemingly no end. "Then we will have an out into the real world at the bottom of the stairs."

"Let's hope you are right." Oka shifted to her smaller shape and leapt once more to my shoulder, perching there easily.

"You must have been a bird in a former life," I said as I took a step down, one hand on the wall the stairs snugged up against and one hand raised, holding the flame.

"This is my first life, so maybe in the next I shall be a bird," she said.

A wind curled up the stairs, dank and stale, and smelling vaguely of old blood.

"You smell that?" Oka's voice, as small as it was, echoed in the tight space.

"Yes." I didn't stop moving. We had to get out of here, and that meant moving forward even if it smelled of death and danger below. "Ever notice that I never get rescued?" I muttered.

"I rescue you," she said.

"I mean . . . like isn't there a point where you want the hero to rescue you?" I found myself smiling, thinking of Mac. "Mac saved my butt a few times, but when it came to the crux of a situation . . ."

"You had to rescue yourself." She bobbed her head. "That is a mark of a strong woman. Not to wait for someone else to lift you, but to start the climb on your own, no matter how tough it is."

She leaned her head against me. "I knew it when I first met you, Pam. When you picked me up, I couldn't see, I had no fur, my body was charred and I was dying. But you saved me. You brought me back to life. In that moment, I knew I would never leave you, because as young as you were, as scared as you were, you faced what came your way head on, helping others along the way."

Her words made my eyes prickle with tears and I didn't have a free hand to dash them away. "Oka, I could never have made it this far without you."

She laughed. "Yes, you would have. You might not have enjoyed the journey as much without my wit and wisdom—"

Now it was my turn to laugh. "Wisdom? As if you are ages older than me?"

"My point is, you would have survived. You bring people to you that can help you, and they want to help you. Like Mac. Like Alex. Like me." Her claws dug into my shoulder as I took a bigger step down, the stairs set farther apart than the upper ones.

"It cost Mac his life," I reminded her as though she needed reminding.

"And he gave it willingly," she said, "as I would if it came to that. As I'm sure Alex would, and perhaps even your father if pushed."

I laughed. "You mean pushed off a cliff?"

Our laughter seemed to shove back the darkness almost more than the light in my hand. I caught a glimpse of the final few steps. They disappeared into water. That was not the same as the castle I remembered.

I grimaced. "I think we're about to get wet."

"Lovely," she muttered. "Perhaps it won't be that deep."

At the last dry step, I held the flame out, making it bigger to see if I could catch a glimpse of the true bottom. Three more stairs, and then floor.

"Well, it looks like you'll stay dry at least." I slid into the water with each step, the liquid cool, but not cold through my clothing. With my feet on the bottom, the water reached mid-chest on me. I let a finger dip into the water and yelped. "Greasy tits on a troll! That is frigid!"

"Are you not feeling it? Wait, it's the clothing you have. It's protecting you again." Oka peered into the water and then dipped a paw. She jerked back with a hiss. "That is cold enough that the water should be solid."

Even as she said that I could feel the water tug on me, as if it were a slushy and not pure liquid. I turned and looked behind us, horror catching in my throat. The water crystalized even as I looked at it.

"The doorway is over there." I held both hands up, lighting them each with a flame. The heat cascaded down on us, but I knew without a shadow of a doubt that flame wouldn't save me if the ice crystals caught us.

I hurried as best I could without slipping a foot on a slick bit of stone. The water grew colder, pushing on the clothing I wore like a compression suit. My clothing—that was the only explanation for why I was not feeling the cold—I'd acquired in the Veil from Fergus. He'd said I'd need its protection for the remainder of my journey.

He was not wrong about that in the least, and a rush of gratitude flowed through me for the smart, four-armed, bespeckled little man.

"Not to stress you out, but please hurry," Oka whispered.

I made the mistake of glancing backward. A slow rolling wave of slushy water curled toward me. Slow, as though it knew it didn't need to hurry in order to freeze me where I was, because I would run out of room soon enough.

I yanked my eyes away from the hypnotizing wave and leaned forward, hurrying as best I could.

"There, I see a door, just ahead and on the left side of the wall!" Oka stood on her back legs, her front legs on top of my head. Which was right where I remembered the door in the original castle. It would lead out of a cave in

New Mexico—or what had been New Mexico, if I was right. If I was wrong, I'd be dead in no time.

I adjusted my stride, pushing hard against the water. It felt like it was a thick mud rather than water, but of course, it wasn't that either. With my hands above my head still, I reached the door. A wide lintel ran across the top, and Oka leapt up and onto it. "I hate to say this, but . . ." She gave me a look.

I already knew, though, what I was going to have to do. And if I took more than a moment to hesitate, I wouldn't do it at all. I drew in a deep breath and jammed one hand under the water, reaching for the knob. My fingers clenched involuntarily against the cold and I had to force them open to wrap around the knob. I twisted hard and pulled, and the door gave a little, but not enough.

"Son of a bitch!" I yelled as I plunged my second hand down into the water, dousing the light. Both hands burned as though I'd shoved them into the coal embers of a fire instead of water. With both hands on the knob, I twisted and pulled, splashing the thick water around me. Droplets flew up and landed on my cheeks, burning me with a sharp icy cold that made me gasp.

"Hurry!" Oka yelled.

I did the only thing I could, knowing this was going to go badly for me. I lifted my feet and put them on the side of the door and pulled with all I had.

7

ALEX

I bowed my head, hands on my hips as I stood there, Wade's words sinking into my brain as my feet sunk into the mud at the back of the caravan. So I'd pissed off the elementals, shown them that we shouldn't be messed with. But I should have killed them? So now what? That was the question of the day.

"Too early for this kind of fuckity shit garbage," I grumbled under my breath.

The caravan rolled to a halt and a shout came from up front.

"We need help! Jimmy's not breathing!"

Wade jogged ahead of me and I followed, slower. We reached the front truck where Jimmy had been. Nathanda, the caravan's nurse, was there, working hard on him.

"What happened?" Richard asked Jimmy's girl, Beth.

"He was sleeping," she held onto his hand tight, "mumbling in his sleep and then he just, he just stopped breathing!" Beth barely held back a sob.

I took a few steps back, knowing that there was nothing I could do. Fight the big fights, make Richard move the caravan, kill an elemental, but here I was just in the way.

A wail of grief rose up a moment later, and I turned to see Nathanda shaking her head. Damn. Something about Jimmy's death didn't sit well with me. He was young, and fit. What had happened?

Richard made quick directions for Jimmy to buried, and for everyone else to set up for a break and then they would head on out again. That was the reality of our world now; death was a daily occurrence and there was no real horror to it anymore, sad as that was.

I'd stood still too long, and a heavy lethargy crept up on me, dragging me down. Everything that had happened the last few hours was catching up.

"I need to sleep before I fall over." I stumbled even as I spoke, as though I were drunk. And maybe I was, more than a little drunk on the power I'd stolen from the sylph. Not that she didn't deserve it.

A pair of hands caught me as I fell to the side. "Holy shit, Alex, did you take a wound?"

Crimson's voice was distant, and all I could do was shake my head. "Sleep."

"Yeah, no kidding, you're like a dead weight." She grabbed me around the waist and the desire to take her to my bed surged upward. I groaned and managed—barely—to stuff the urge down.

I don't know for sure if Crimson felt anything, but she did hurry me up, getting me to a spot clear of the main traffic of people. "Shift and sleep here. We'll keep watch. Was there anything behind us besides the rain?"

"Not anymore," I mumbled.

Her words sunk into me and I obeyed her as if I were still a submissive. Once more on four legs, I crumpled to the ground and curled myself into a ball, my tail flipping over my face for good measure. I think I'd shook my head, in response to her question, but maybe not. Besides, technically they were still back there, still chasing us. If what Wade had said was correct.

Sleep swallowed me down and I fell into it with a bliss-filled sigh.

I don't know how long I was out, or how long it took me to realize I was dreaming, but there I was, in a dream.

Had to be, because there was Pamela staring back at me, her blue eyes wide. That new silver streak in her hair beckoning to me to touch it.

"Alex." She walked toward me, eyes full of uncertainty. And because it was a dream, I didn't worry about what my incubus power would do, if it would try and drink her down, because this was just a dream. Touching her here was safe. Maybe more than touching her if this dream was a real good one.

I caught her up and pulled her into a hug, crushing her to my chest. A sob rippled out of her, and she clung to me, her fingers digging in hard as if she would never let me go. "I can't find my way out," she said. "Where am I?"

"I don't know where you are," I murmured against her hair. "But you're here with me and that is the way it's supposed to be." Gods, she smelled good, like summer sweet flowers and new grass and something else I couldn't quite put my finger on, something spicy, something that made my blood run a little hotter. I rubbed my hands up her back, letting my fingers play along her spine, learning her body.

There was no one else there, just her and me. Not Oka even. Gods, this kind of a dream would get me into trouble, that was for sure. I didn't care. I pulled my shirt over my head and she blinked up at me but didn't stop me from stripping.

Her clothes quickly followed and her skin was against mine. This was more than I'd imagined, and even though it was just a dream, I didn't care. Her mouth pressed against mine, her hands roamed my body and we tumbled to the ground. Hands on her hips, I pulled her onto me, and tipped my head back as I slid into her. "Goddess."

"Yes?" She smiled down at me, her eyes sparkling. I laughed up at her.

"Full of yourself, aren't you?"

She took my hands and slid them up over her breasts as she began to move on top of me. "I am your goddess, am I not?"

"Yes. Every day." I tried to sit up to kiss her, and she shoved me back down with one hand and pinned me there.

"Stay where you are put, Alex." Her eyes flashed and she shifted her weight, keeping my attention on her body, and what she was doing to me. My breath came in gulps and I wanted her to slow down. To give her more pleasure than just this moment. Even if it was a dream. It was a dream, wasn't it?

It did not feel like a dream. I slid my hands up over the

curve of her waist and let my power trickle through her, not to take her energy, but to give her more. She gasped, her eyelids fluttered closed, and then a slow moan fell from her lips. "What are you doing?"

She trembled under my hands and pulled my power back a little, sliding it between us, running it over her—

"Alex, what are you doing?" She struggled as she seemed to see me for the first time. But that couldn't be the case. It couldn't.

I frowned and pulled my power back further. Now in my dreams she was going to turn me down too? I blew out a breath and twisted up my lips. "I'm going to make you enjoy this."

She closed her eyes and rocked forward hard and fast, catching me by surprise. I put my hands on her to stop her, and she smacked them away. "I'll finish this," she whispered.

I couldn't help it, my body followed her, and the pleasure peaked in me. Everything I'd wanted with her, and yet there was so much missing. Besides the fact that it was a dream.

She rolled from me, snapped her fingers and her clothing was back on her, as if she'd never taken it off. I followed suit slowly.

"Pam?" I reached for her and she shook her head.

"Don't call me that."

I laughed and brushed a hand under her jaw. "That's your name."

She batted my hand away and again there was a flash in her eyes I didn't like. I swallowed hard.

Oka, in her tiger form, stalked toward us through the

mist of the dream. "Alex, what the hell are you doing here? Are you stuck too?"

I looked from Oka to Pam and back again. "Wait . . . I'm dreaming. Aren't I? I went to sleep and woke up here."

Pamela blinked a few times as if we'd not just fucked in the middle of this place, apparently with Oka only a few feet away. "You might be dreaming, but we are trapped here."

"Holy shit, are you kidding me? Seriously, you barely get out of one trap and you walk right into another?" Perhaps that wasn't the best way to go about expressing myself, but I never claimed to be brilliant around women —especially Pam. And I was confused between the lust raging still in my body, the love, and the fear for whatever the crown of darkness was that she was supposed to have to deal with.

Her mouth thinned and her eyes narrowed. "Not really the time, Alex."

"I'm just saying!" I threw my hands in the air. "Not that I'm not glad to see you since you decided to just run off and leave me behind with the caravan. As if . . ." As if she didn't care for me.

"You think that's going to soften her toward you?" Oka shook her head.

"It's the truth," I said.

"That doesn't mean I *wanted* to leave you behind. Every man I've loved has been killed, Alex. Does that mean nothing to you?" She paced in front of me, the strange mists around us billowing up with each step. "Do you not see that I'm protecting you and the caravan? I'm a danger to you. I will not be coming back. You need to get that through your thick head."

I threw my hands into the air a second time, frustrated. "Please, you're doing like you always do, running from what scares you. I know I scare you, Pam. I know that what is between us scares you and has since the moment I saw you after all those years apart."

Her pacing stopped and she raised her hands to her face, covering her eyes. Shit.

I put a hand on her shoulder, half expecting Oka to take a swipe at me and surprised when she didn't. Very carefully I turned Pam toward me and moved her hands from her face. Tears streamed down her cheeks and those blue eyes that I'd dreamed of for so long swam with her emotions. "I'm sorry. For everything."

"It's only going to get darker from here, Alex. I can feel it growing, and I don't know that even I know. When I'm awake. When I'm asleep. Does that make sense?" She stared up at me and I was sure it was her, the girl I loved.

"You're right," she whispered. "I am scared. I've always loved you, Alex. First as my friend, and then as more because you were all I had to hang onto when I was on my own. I thought you'd find me. But I loved Mac too, and look at what happened to him. Look at what me loving people does to their lives. Oka has nearly died how many times? My brother has been kidnapped, my father cut off from his power for years. And now . . . the darkness is so dark and so strong, and I can't . . . I need it." She clamped her mouth shut as if there was something else, something she couldn't bring herself to say.

"Not all of that is your fault." I lowered her hands and

once more pulled her into my arms, albeit with a little less passion than before. A sigh slid from her and she leaned into me, resting her face against my chest. "You have to fight the darkness, Pam. You have to."

She ignored part of what I'd said. "Much of it is my fault. Because I thought I knew what I was doing. I'm stuck here now." She let me take some of her weight, let me hold her tight.

As suddenly as she leaned into me, she shoved away, her eyes blazing. "You won't have her much longer. She can't fight me forever, and I can see her heart. I can see what will make her do as I wish."

The voice was husky, deep.

That was not my Pam.

I looked at Oka. But her eyes were closed and she breathed deeply. "Oka doesn't know, does she?"

"No, and when the moment comes, she will die. To solidify my hold on this one." She smiled. "She's mine."

Pam blinked and Oka opened her eyes. I reached for her and she stumbled back. "No, I can't trust you. I can't trust that you won't try and take my power again."

What the hell?

I swallowed hard, knowing that trying to convince her would be futile. I forced a smile, forced words to come from my mouth.

"Well, if I'm dreaming, which I'm pretty sure I am, then you just need to wake up," I said.

She looked at me and I looked down and shit if I could remember what else I was going to say. Because all I wanted was to taste those lips of hers, to strip her clothes off and kiss every inch of her from the curve of her calves to the crook of her neck. A different kind of heat rose between us, different than when I was taking the life of the sylph, different than the heat between Jasmine and me.

I took a chance. She didn't seem to remember that we'd been naked, our bodies joined, only moments before. But a kiss, a kiss with my girl, maybe it would be like the fairy tales.

"Maybe you just need incentive to wake up." I bent and pressed my lips against hers, sliding my tongue into her mouth and tasting her just as I'd wanted. Sweet, she was sweet but there was a dark spice there too that drew me in deeper. Damn it all, I wanted this to be real, but I wanted it to be a dream too so I could have my way with her and not feel bad when I woke.

That dark spice that was all Pamela flooded my senses and I checked my incubus power but it was quiet, resting. Maybe it was silent when I dreamed. I didn't know and didn't care. I deepened the kiss and Pamela let me lead as I angled my mouth against hers, as I slid my hands around her back under her cloak, and down over the curve of her ass, tugging her body close to mine.

Reluctantly, I pulled my head back, my breath coming in gulps as I pressed my forehead against hers. "So that didn't work. Maybe we should try again."

Pamela pushed me away, her eyes wild with fear. "No more, not until you learn to control yourself."

I hadn't taken a drop of her power, yet she believed I had. Just like that, the penny dropped and I understood. Whatever she was seeing was not what was real. Her perception was completely skewed.

"Idiots, the pair of you," Oka muttered. "Kissing her is not going to wake her up."

"Works in fairy tales." I forced a grin as I tried to think of how to snap her out of this. Something between us lightened the darkness. She laughed again.

"This is no fairy tale, Alex."

"Sure it is. There's bad guys chasing the good guys. A handsome prince." I winked down at her and she blushed and shook her head. "And a beautiful girl in trouble again. Mind you, the beautiful girl doesn't likely need saving like most fairy tales. But you do have an animal sidekick who is mouthy on the best of days. So you see, fairy tale."

Oka grunted. "I am not a sidekick."

Pam grinned and then the smile slid from her face as her brows furrowed. She didn't pull away from me as we stood there, but I could feel the pull toward the caravan. Someone shook me in the waking world and was trying to wake me.

"Pam, I've got to go." I kissed her lightly again, just a pressing of our lips together, no matter how badly I wanted to taste her again . . . okay maybe I tugged that soft lower lip of hers into my mouth for a last nip, wishing I could indeed wake her from this nightmare with a simple kiss.

"You can figure this out. You just have to wake up." I didn't just mean the place she was stuck in either, and the flash in her eyes told me that the other part of her knew exactly what I was getting at.

She held tightly to me, but I was slipping away, even though I didn't want to. I wanted to stay there with her, where I was supposed to be. I let her go, because I didn't know what else to do.

A hand on my shoulder shook me harder. "Wake up, dude. Damn it, you sleep like the dead, you know that?"

I pulled my tail from across my face and blinked up at Wade as he stared down at me. I cracked a yawn, stood and stretched with my front paws out, head down, butt in the air. "What's happening?"

"Richard is having problems. No one saw the elementals but you and me, and that Chris woman is wanting to go back to the ravine." He shook his head. "She can't seem to grasp just what happened back there, that there is nothing left."

I groaned and shifted back to two legs though I still sat on the ground. My clothing was rumpled and there was a tear in my shirt that I didn't remember getting—maybe that was sloppy shifting on my part.

I pushed to my feet, yawned again and Wade snickered. "Good dreams?"

I glanced down and shifted my pants, trying to push down the desire Pamela had called up in me. "Something like that. Why again am I dealing with this? Why is Richard not just telling her that it's not possible?"

Wade grimaced. "I may have told them that you battled the three elementals, and now they think you're a mage."

My feet stuttered to a stop. "You what?"

He shrugged. "They would not understand why it's good to keep an incubus on our side, but magic they grasp —at least a little. So for now, it looks like you, my friend, are our caravan witch."

Well, damn, that was not what I was expecting to wake

up to. But maybe it would help me keep the caravan safer if they were willing to listen to me—if they were willing to follow me as they'd followed Pam. At least until I found the big trees Peta mentioned.

I licked my lips, and thought I could still taste Pamela on them, that sweet darkness that called to me to bury myself in her, again, in every way possible. For her I would do this. I would keep dealing with the idiots to keep the caravan safe. That was all there was to it.

And I would trust her to find her way, to deal with what she had to deal with. Trust that she would come back to me. That whatever crown of darkness waited, she would be strong enough to push it away, to hang onto the light.

As I approached the center of the caravan the raised voices told a far better story than if someone had sat me down and explained what I was walking into.

This was about to get really interesting.

8

PAMELA

Deep in the dungeon of the castle, we were in more than a little bit of trouble as I fought to get Oka and myself out and back into the real world. I tried to connect with the freezing water that wrapped around me, to push it away, to buy us time, but this place of dreams was having none of that. I might as well have spit at the water for whatever change I made in it with my power. As I pulled with my arms and pushed with my legs on either side of the stubborn doorway, our only way out of this dreamscape, I knew it was now or never. And never would mean that Oka and I would both die here, in the frigid cold waters in the belly of the castle, lost from the waking world. My family would die, the caravan would lose its way, Frost would be lost to the elementals.

I refused to allow that to happen. I screamed as I pulled on the door, one last heave of strength going into opening it.

The doorway gave and I was pulling hard enough that I went under the water completely.

I'd never been in water so cold, never felt it drive into me so that my instincts took over and I had no conscious thought about how to handle it. The desire to get out of the cold took over and I shot to the surface, my head aching as though I'd smashed it into the wall and not fallen into the water.

Oka was yelling and then she was on my shoulder, headbutting me. "MOVE!"

I stumbled forward, started to go down again into the water and then sloshed forward and through the open door. There was darkness on the other side and I didn't care, I just kept moving, my brain mush in the cold. I slid downward again, and then I was in the water, darkness all around me, and I was kicking toward the surface of something.

The water wasn't as cold, at least there was that, and the pain in my head and hands receded a little, though I'm ashamed to admit I lost complete control of my bladder, warmth running down my legs. How was that even possible? I was cold, not hit in the belly by a troll or something. I broke the surface of the water and found my feet easily. It was only then that I realized I stood in water that was barely a foot deep inside a shallow cave. I stumbled out of the puddle, and Oka clawed her way out after me.

My legs shook so hard that I could barely stand, and ended up bent at the waist, just breathing through the shock of the cold, still unable to control my bladder. My hands were a bright red and I had no doubt my face would be the same. Like a sunburn, only a cold burn.

The air around us was still, the sun outside shaded with clouds and not a single tree or bush near us. A wasteland lay around us—even the smell was stale as if nothing moved here, nothing lived. But I could feel the difference—we were back in the real world. There was that at least.

"Oka, you okay?" My words were mumbled, thick as though I was half asleep, or drunk.

"Wet and cold," she said, shaking herself and licking at a few drops of water on her shoulder. "But the worst of the frigid water hit you, I think."

I nodded. "Let's go," I said as I reached for spirit and wove the spell that would allow me to jump the Veil away from where we'd stumbled out. I motioned for Oka to come to me and she sprang into my arms as I completed the spell. Only I didn't try and take us to Frost. I didn't even try to take us to Raven. I thought of the edge of Raven's home, of the swamp he'd dragged us through.

In a split second we were there, standing in the swamp, in the slightly warm water, Raven's eyes bugging out as we appeared before him. We'd been gone not long, an hour maybe?

"Hi." I lifted a cold burned hand. "Sorry about that."

"How the hell did you get out of there?" He strode toward me and pulled me out of the water and, surprisingly, into a hug that squeezed the air out of me, warmth flooding from him into me, driving the last of the cold away.

"Umm, you knew where I was?" I pulled back and realized that he'd once again healed my wounds. My hands and face no longer hurt, just the memory of the cold made me shudder.

"In theory." He shook his head. "It is a place of limbo that traps those foolish enough to try and jump the Veil to somewhere they are forbidden. A punishment, if you will. How did you get out?" He frowned at me, confusion written across his face as plain as day.

"She used the door like any sensible woman would," Oka bit out. "Although it was a tad bit wet."

He shot a look at Oka. "There are no doorways in limbo."

I shrugged, bothered by how confused he was—he was supposed to have the answers, not be confused by what I was capable of. "What can I say? There was a castle like the one that used to be a central point of the Veil, so I used it the same way and found a doorway out. Though I think if it happened again, I would try another doorway. That one sucked."

Raven grabbed my arms, his fingers tight on my biceps. "Promise me you will not try this again. Jumping through the Veil to a person is dangerous. That is why I tried to get you to stop once I realized you were capable."

Oka reached up and patted my hand. "What he means is he went and researched what you did after he saw you could jump directly to a person years ago. That is what he is saying."

Raven nodded. "Oka is correct. I had never heard of anyone being able to jump the Veil directly to a person. I found some old texts and they warned of the dangers of doing so. Unless you are absolutely certain that the person you are jumping to won't be within a safe haven, it is damn dangerous." His hands were still on my arms. "Only one other person was able to escape that limbo, and write about it."

"Lark?" I asked.

He shook his head. "No, though you'd think so with all she did in her short life." He kept a hand on me, and I felt him weave spirit around us, taking us somewhere else. I closed my eyes because for just a flash I was afraid of what would happen. What if me going into the limbo would make it so I was pulled back there again and again? I didn't want to go back there, to see the nightmares come to life once more.

The world wobbled around us for a split second, then solidified just as fast.

My feet sunk into soft ground, waves rolling up along a long stretch of black sand beach. The salty air curled around, and into me, the freshness of it cleansing every part of me. I breathed it in deeply, and the inherent power in the water called to me. I held out my hands and drew that power in, let it flow through my veins, whispering to me of tsunamis and crashing waves, of ocean currents and all the life within it. At least the water here listened to me.

"Raven, I've never felt the water like this before," I whispered, unable to stop the flow of the power through me, and not wanting to.

He didn't answer, and I slowly turned to him, struggling to stop whatever this was I was feeling even though I didn't want to. "Raven?"

Those blue eyes of his were unreadable. "I don't know, Pam, what you're feeling."

A voice rolled up around us, deep and resonating, warm and safe. The Mother Goddess spoke to us both. *"She is ready for more. She will be the balance."*

A smile crept over my lips, but slid as Raven closed his eyes, his head lowered, and his chin touched his chest. "No. She is not ready for this. Don't take her from me."

Just those simple words and it was as though I was thrown back into the icy waters below the castle that I'd only just escaped. "No?"

"You cannot be the balance." His words were sharp. "You are not strong enough."

I'd have been less shocked if he'd slapped me. Before I could ask another question, he snapped his fingers at me to follow him, and his voice was hard. "We are meeting with the undines. I am hoping to sway them to tell us where Frost is. Use spirit on them if you can."

"Likely difficult for me since I'm so weak," I shot back.

His body stiffened and a tremor rolled through him. "Not the time, *daughter*."

"It never is the time for anything that I need. Don't worry, I'll figure it out. Eventually. All by myself," I said, barely able to keep the pain from my voice. So much for thinking my father believed in me, that he supported me.

Truth.

"I'm here; you aren't by yourself." Oka's warmth was all I had and I leaned into her, wishing for Mac. Wishing he could come back, that he could be at my side again.

"Not Alex?" Oka asked.

The sand pulled at my feet as I followed Raven along the shoreline. "I . . . I love them both. I would rather lose them because they walked away than because of them dying. But I would choose Mac. I think." I shook my head.

Below my feet, through the soles of my boots, the warmth of the earth and the call of the ocean warred for my attention. The Mother Goddess believed in me, that would have to be enough for now. Her power was warm, a heat that told me she would be with me forever.

I blew out a breath and looked down the shoreline as figures emerged from the water, walking as though they'd walked along the ocean's bottom through the depths. A half dozen of them, hair color of green, blue, pale purple, bodies lithe for the swimmers they were, eyes as deep as the ocean they were from.

Undines, water elementals. I swallowed hard, thinking of my last fight to free myself from the bands that held me from my power, from the undine that I'd killed in order to have my power back.

"Easy," Oka whispered. "You were not in the wrong. They were."

Raven stopped about twenty feet from the group of undines. "Cousins."

One of the undines stood ahead of the others and I was sure he was the king. But he was young, my age, maybe a year or two older. His hair was short, cut back into a messy blue spike across his head where the others had hair past their shoulders. His eyes were dark, almost black in their depths.

"We are no cousins of yours, Raven." Those dark eyes swung to me and I tipped my chin up, refusing to look away. I would not be intimidated by an undine, king or not.

"I am looking for a child," Raven went on, maybe oblivious to the fact that the young king was no longer looking at him. "A fair-haired child of blue eyes, barely three years old."

"A child of the rending, your child?" another of the undines asked. "An elemental child? We know of no child."

Of course they were lying. The smirks on their faces, the glitter in their eyes, the sly looks to each other. The pieces of shit were lying and loving it. Loving that they would hurt Raven. And even though my father was being a dick to me at the moment, nobody else was allowed to do that to him. I started to weave spirit, blending it with my blood magic.

I would show them who they were tangling with and just what the cost would be. Anger shot through me, not the anger of being caged, not the anger of wanting to get even . . . anger that they would make innocents suffer for their own desires.

That was unacceptable.

A thin tendril of my magic was all I needed to get the attention of the young king. A pulse of energy, tasting of the ocean and heat of the earth, and his eyes swung my way. A pull on his desires.

From the corner of my eye, Raven nodded as if he would take the undines at their word. "If you hear of anything, a whisper, I would be grateful of you—" He startled as the young king walked past him to stand in front of me. The urge to call the power of the ocean to me and thrash him with it, to show him just how strong I was, swept over me. I held back, feeding him a little of my magic, not enough to make him aware, just enough to make him want me.

Yes, seduce him, make him want to fuck you and you will have him on his knees. Sam nodded. *Men can be led by their passions, do it.*

"Who are you?" the king asked. "I can feel the ocean in your veins, but you are no undine."

Raven was silent, and I realized then that he would not claim me as his daughter, not even when I was trying to help find Frost. Was he embarrassed by me? Was he ashamed that he had a half-breed daughter?

Pain I didn't realize I had left in me reared its head, cutting through the warmth I'd thought I had for my father. Below my feet and in the water around us, there was strength, there was love from the Mother Goddess. I looked the young king in the eye and raised a brow.

"My name is Pamela, and I am the Mother Goddess's balance. And just who are you?"

An echo of indrawn air rippled through the undines. The king's night-dark eyes widened and a slight smile quirked over his lips. "I am the king of the undines."

"A nameless king? Not very original," I said.

A laugh rippled from him. "You have not earned my real name. So King will do just fine."

He lifted a hand as if he would touch me and a low snarl rippled from Oka on my shoulder. "Not if you like your fingers where they are attached, pup."

If I thought he couldn't be more surprised, I was wrong. "You have a familiar from the Pit?"

"I do."

"But you are not an elemental."

86

"No."

He frowned. "I do not understand."

I wove spirit quickly now, banking on his lack of attention. "Where is the child, King? Where is the little boy hidden away?"

His eyes fluttered to half-mast and a low sigh slid out of his lips. "The sylphs have him."

"No, do not tell them!" one of the undines yelled. "You are be-spelled! You know how to fight this!"

"Then I will be be-spelled," he murmured. "Her power is like nothing I've ever felt."

I took a step back, but didn't let go of spirit as I wove it faster and harder around him. But it wasn't just spirit, it was the magic in my blood—it was Sam blending with the elemental power that was working through the king of the undines.

"Let him go," Raven commanded. "That is not how we do things here."

"Where are the sylphs hiding?" I demanded the answer from the king and he went to his knees, his head thrown back. The urge to touch him, to delve my fingers under his skin and feel his very life against me rose hot and urgent.

I clenched my hands into fists. "Tell me."

"The broken mountains," he whispered. "They are there, hiding from you. Keeping the child."

I kept my power on him, riding him hard, and felt something inside his head. I was not the first with spirit to have entered his mind. Someone was controlling him. "Will they harm the child?"

His body jerked, and an image of Frost being smacked,

of him crying in a corner slammed into my brain. I couldn't stop the gasp at the cruelty they would show a child, an innocent child!

The undines yelled, the ocean behind us frothed and a creature shot out, tentacles reaching for the king, grabbing him around the legs and yanking him away from me into the water. Gone, he was gone, but I had my answer. Frost was being hurt.

My rage knew no bounds at the thought of my little brother's blue eyes scared and full of pain, of tears tracking those baby-soft cheeks. I did a slow turn, letting the anger fill me, letting it override any other sense in me.

No one hurts one of my own. It was Sam's voice, but it was my thought.

"Raven!" The undine with the purple hair snarled, "You have broken the accord. You agreed that to use spirit was a death sentence! She will die."

"No, *I* agreed to it. She did not!" Raven snarled right back.

Oka dropped from my shoulder and shifted to her tiger form. "I believe we are about to get in a tangle."

The five undines remaining stood on the black sand, not moving, but I could feel their power driving through the ocean, stirring it up. A burst of water shot from the ocean's surface and began to spin, lazy at first, then faster and faster.

"We leave, to my home!" Raven looked back at me as he gave the command, and then he disappeared, gone in a flash as he jumped the Veil.

Only I didn't want to go. These undines were dangerous. They were taking children, hurting them, controlling their people through a puppet.

If I was the Mother Goddess's balance, then it was time to show the elementals they were not the top of the food chain.

I was.

9

The funnel on the ocean spun closer to me, salt spray whipping across my face and tangling my long hair around my face, but I didn't move. If the undines wanted a fight I would give them a fight, even here at the ocean's edge where their power was strongest. I widened my stance to hold against the buffeting of the funnel as I stared at the undines. "You have the king as your puppet. He will break free, and then you will see what damage you've done."

"He will never break free," the purple-haired undine said.

I raised a hand and flicked my fingers toward the ocean, feeling for the king, for where the pulse of spirit lay inside his head. Using my own connection to the water, I pulled him out of the depths to the surface.

They didn't seem to notice. They were focused on me and the funnel. The water lapped at my feet and I started forward as the undines rushed me, weapons drawn from their sides. Long pikes, a whip, trident, and a net scattered with barbed hooks.

I didn't go for my blades; they were too short. Instead I sent a ripple of power through the earth under their feet, opening the black sand and sucking them down. I didn't hesitate but shoved them as deeply as I could.

"That won't hold them," Oka said.

"I know, but I need a moment." I turned away from the buried undines, feeling them struggle against my power, knowing they would break free in moments. Already the ground split above them as the water rushed in toward them, softening the sand. With them distracted, the funnel faded. I pulled the young king across the top of the water all the way to me, dropping him at my feet.

I cupped his face and sent a burst of energy into him even as I unraveled the hold on his mind, the connection to spirit that was keeping him in thrall to the other undines.

And I saw who'd put it there.

Raven.

My heart thumped hard, fear and confusion rocking me. Why had my father helped the undines place this one under their control? The young king's jet-black eyes opened and stared up at me. Anger raged through them and I smiled, feeling the strain on my mouth, feeling the hurt in that smile. I delved deeper into his mind and saw something more, something that made me gasp.

A snow-white polar bear looking back at me. Under my hands, the king's body shifted, and Mac was there, standing in front of me.

"Impossible!"

He shook his big head side to side. "I never wanted to leave you, Pam. And I found a way back. Trapped inside this young king until you freed me."

"How, how is this possible?" I stuttered over the words, my shock and joy mingling to make a mess of me.

I didn't understand how Mac could be the young undine king. He shifted back to two legs, and it was the undine once more. But my heart was clamoring, beating as if it would escape out of my chest. I stared down at him.

"Are you done being controlled?"

He stood slowly, taller than me by a good four inches, the same as Mac. I couldn't stop the tremors. "They had my mind warped?"

"They did."

"And you freed me?" He touched a hand to his head. "Why?"

"Because they bound me too. I would leave no one in chains if I have the power to release them." That was the truth. I would not leave someone else bound like that.

I didn't ask him why they chained him, and maybe I should have. I didn't ask him how he'd gained Mac's spirit, and maybe I should have asked that too.

Later. I'd ask later.

He held a hand out to me. "I am in your debt."

"And I am calling that debt in now, King," I said. "The sylphs have my brother. I need to find him and you know where he is."

"No, there is only one person who knows where he is, where the broken mountains are," he said. "There is a terraling that holds the information."

If I thought I'd been shocked and confused before, it was nothing to my reaction to this statement. "What? No, that can't be. The sylphs and undines have made this fight."

"It can be. It is all four families who are in on this." He didn't get to say any more because the other undines broke out of their sand prison.

They crawled out, weapons drawn, sand clinging to their skin. "My liege, she speaks lies," the purple-haired male undine said.

"I think not, Rork," the king said. He lifted his hand and a wave washed in and scooped up Rork. I didn't think that he'd be able to hurt another undine using water.

I was wrong.

The water spun around Rork, encasing him in a bubble. Each rotation he was spun, his body seemed to bloat. It took me a moment to realize what the king was doing. The same trick that the sylphs used on their enemies, shoving air in or out of their body until they imploded or exploded. Rork's body expanded, the skin stretching until there was no more room. I couldn't look away, the horror of it resonating in my soul.

"You will never bind me again," King said. "Never, I will *never* be bound by the likes of you."

He flexed his hand and I felt the power course through him—he was stronger than any other undine I'd met, and that strength could be used. That strength could help me do what I had to do. More than that . . . he wouldn't die. Mac was somehow in him, and he wouldn't die.

A flicker of concern rolled through Oka to me, but I let her see the image they'd shown me of Frost, bleeding, hurt, a little boy crying for comfort. A snarl ripped out of her. And then I let her see the image of Mac. I thought she'd seen him as a polar bear shifter, but maybe that was just an image I'd seen.

Either way, she gasped again. "Impossible," she whispered. But impossible was not a word I reacted well to.

I reached over and took King's hand, giving him a burst of my own power to use. His fingers tightened over mine and together, we pulled Rork apart. The water exploded like a macabre firework, spreading a bright bloom of red through the orb.

"Never again," I whispered. "I won't lose you again. I won't let them hurt my family any more."

The other undines just stared for a moment and then they came at us, en masse.

I could have sucked them into the earth as I'd done before, but I was so angry, I was crying. I wanted nothing to do with these creatures. I didn't want to be like them.

And they needed to learn their place.

There needed to be balance to all the power they held. They needed to stop hurting and imprisoning people. That rage shot through the elemental magic in me, strengthening it. Sam was quiet as I wove my two magics together, making them so strong that no one would ever hurt me again. That no one would hurt Mac, or Oka, or Frost.

No more, I wasn't going to let them hurt me anymore.

A flick of my hand and the wind around us ripped forward, picking them up in a unit. I yanked the air from their lungs, dragging it away until bones cracked and their bodies folded in on themselves.

The whole fight—if you want to call it that—was over in a matter of seconds. Seconds, and I'd destroyed five lives. I shook, for what I'd just done. "Goddess, I am so sorry," I whispered, going to my knees. The young king dropped beside me. The image of his face softened and Mac's blue eyes smiled at me.

"I am here, Pamela. You did what you had to do."

I clung to his hand. "How, how are you here?"

He sighed and cupped my face. "I was an elemental's familiar, Pamela. Even after death, I can be reborn somewhere else. But it seems with the breaking of the world, things got screwy. Instead of ending up as a familiar, I ended up inside the elemental I was supposed to help. His mind is slipping, and it won't be long before he will be gone."

"And you?" I whispered.

"I will not leave." He bent down and kissed me gently and all the love in my heart spilled upward. "The Mother Goddess did not think you should be without two familiars, I think."

I laughed, but the laugh turned into tears. He tucked me close to him. "We need to go, Pam. Can you get us out of here? I will let the boy have his time with this body, a little longer. Then I will take over," Mac said, and then he faded and the undine king looked down at me in his arms. His eyebrows raised.

With a flex of my hand, I flung the crushed bodies out over the land, away from the water that might revive them. "Yes, you're right, we need to go."

"Is Raven your father?" King asked.

I tensed, hating that my own father was embarrassed

by me, that he wasn't willing to tell the other elementals just who I was.

"People judge me for my father too," King said, tightening his hand on mine. "They think I will be the monster he was."

"We have to go." I put my free hand on Oka and wove spirit around the three of us, scooting us away from the black sand beach, toward the mountains in the north. There was a lake Oka and I had stayed at for a few weeks on our journey. No one else knew where it was—at least I was hoping that was still the case. I needed a few minutes to think, to plan what I was going to do next. Did I try to find Raven again? Did I want to be rejected by him again?

King gasped as the world solidified once more. "Did you jump the Veil? Where are we?"

We stood on the shoreline of a brilliant blue lake, the water crystalline, sharp, cold and empty of life. There were no fish in it, nothing grew there. Which was why Oka and I hadn't stayed here, as beautiful as it was. "We are where Raven will not find us. Where the elementals should not find us."

"They are still hunting you?"

I nodded, tired even though the day had only just started, as if I were fighting off a sickness. "They want me dead. Apparently." I tried to pull my hand from his, but he was having none of it. I sighed. "King—if that's what you want me to call you—you know where the child is?"

His dark eyes swept the area and he flexed his fingers, his shoulders rippled not unlike how I'd seen Mac's ripple. The lake was silent and still. He sighed. "There is a well of power here, did you know that?"

I looked at Oka and she wrinkled her nose. When we'd come here before I'd been blocked from my elemental powers by the bands on my wrists. We'd stayed here longer than anywhere else, leaving only when the cold got too much, and the food scarce. "I have always been drawn to this place."

Warmth rose through my feet, soothing me, the Mother Goddess whispering through me. *I created it for you.*

"Mac," I said softly, "if you're in there, can you get him to answer the question?"

He turned back to me, away from the lake, and I thought I saw a flicker of blue in his eyes, there and gone. "Again, I do not have that information, and you are free to look inside my mind to see that I am not lying." He still didn't let go of my hand, his fingers massaging across my knuckles. Something Mac would do. "Go ahead, I know you want to make sure. I know that you do not trust me, with reason."

The thing was, I did trust him, because Mac—whatever made up his soul—was in there. Maybe I should have been warier, but I couldn't bring myself to not trust him. I shot a look at Oka. She shrugged with a big roll of her shoulders. Her thoughts came through loud and clear. He would not be able to fight me if I used spirit on him, so it was as safe as we were going to get.

Cautiously, I lifted a hand, and put it against his cheek. Stubble under my fingers, and the coolness of the ocean cascaded down my arm. I closed my eyes. This man was strength, he was power, and ambition, he was fierce and ready to fight . . . and under that, the roar of a bear, the cold of the Arctic and the bite of snow against me.

He was nothing like Alex.

I could have Mac again. He could be in my life. We'd get a second chance.

Pain flared around my heart thinking of Alex, thinking of him on his own forever.

Perhaps, Sam said softly, as if from a distance. *Do not fall for this one, though. He is dangerous, I think.*

"Who hurt you, my witch?" he said, and his voice blurred into Mac's.

My witch. His hand covered mine and he leaned into me as if he would close the distance between us and try to kiss me, and part of me wanted that. Part of me wanted to feel Mac alive and in my arms. I wanted to ask him again what he'd meant about the Mother Goddess giving him a second chance, about how he'd come to be in the undine's body.

He smiled at me. "Blood speaks to blood. Are you happy with what you see in my mind?"

I hadn't even delved him yet. I pushed a tendril of spirit into him and saw there was no real knowledge of where Frost was—he knew only that the sylphs held the little boy. And there again was the image of Mac, the polar bear shifter who'd stolen my heart and shown me it was okay to love. I tightened my hold on him for just a moment, the need for him stronger than ever before.

"I am not an undine, we do not carry the same blood. But I think you carry something of mine." I carefully extricated my hand from his and stepped back, needing space to breathe. To think. "I AM an elemental witch,

King. I am shunned by both sides of my—" I paused because I didn't want to say family. *Blood* seemed too crass . . .

"I understand," he said softly. "Perhaps more than you realize." He shrugged and put his palm out over the ground. A tiny seedling popped up, reaching for his hand. "No one knows I am a half-breed, that I have a connection to the earth."

And suddenly the reason why Mac would be able to be part of his life, or to be sent to him as a familiar, made sense. Mac was a land shifter. King was part terraling.

"You tell your secrets too easily," Oka said. "You are young and need a familiar to keep you in check."

I bit back a smile, realizing she didn't know yet that Mac was with him. "Who then? You said a terraling knows where the boy is. Who is it that knows?"

I shouldn't have been surprised by the name, but it still hurt. Because she was family, and I thought maybe my family was done betraying me.

"Belladonna, queen of the terralings."

I didn't want to believe that King was right about Belladonna. She was not only the queen of the terralings, but she was my aunt, Raven's sister. I'd met her when I was younger, and she had seemed kind . . . I couldn't believe that she would be party to hurting a child.

"No, that can't be." I shook my head, horror flickering through me. "She wouldn't."

"She would and she has. You have a naïve view on how the elemental world works if you believe that they would not kill a child they see as a threat. It is why I have kept silent about my dual abilities. It is why they try to kill you over and over. Why they hate Raven. They are purists. The boy, he has dual abilities, does he not?"

I nodded, knowing he was not wrong. "His mother is a sylph. I don't know how many abilities he inherited from Raven."

"Then that is what you must understand, that he is seen as a threat—even as a child, and easier to remove as a child. Do they want another Raven? Another you? If they could have killed any of us as children, they would have. If they could have, they would have killed Lark too. They hate her for what she did to the world." King's words were harsh and they cut into me worse than a stranger's words should have, because with each word I could hear Mac come through stronger.

I turned my face from him. "You . . . you can't know these things. You think they would truly kill him? He's a sweet little boy."

"I do believe it, and it will only be a matter of time until they do it. I've lived their rules and didn't do well with it, my witch. It is partially why they bound me. They were scared of me. Even without my ability with the earth, I am the strongest undine that they have ever seen. My father was a monster, powerful, but a monster, and my abilities eclipse his. My mother did all she could to protect me as a child. They thought she was my nanny and they . . . they killed her to keep me in line." He stepped up to stand beside me, looking out over the lake. "I can't see in your mind like you can see in mine, but I see the pain in your body. I see the scars and I feel like I've known you in another life. We can help each other, I think."

His words brought tears to my eyes. Mac, that was my Mac speaking. "What do you need help from me for?"

"To make sure they don't warp my mind again." His hands tightened into fists. "You can do that, can't you? You can keep them out of my head? I would stay with you for that alone, if not for your beauty and strength."

A shiver ran through me, certainty flooding me. "Yes, I

can do that. But it will take time and safety, neither of which we have right now."

He nodded. "And the cost to me?"

"Help me save Frost. He's my little brother and does not deserve to be hurt, or killed, or kept from those who love him. That's torture." I shook my head, fighting with the emotions that rolled through me. I had to keep it together. I had to stay strong for Frost. And then for Rylee. I had to go to Rylee and stop the elementals from hurting her. I knew what it was to be kept from those you loved.

"I can do that. I feel like this was meant to be, my witch." He held out a hand and the image that superimposed over him was Mac in the flesh. He winked at me and I smiled, though my lips wobbled. I couldn't help it. I loved him and would love him no matter how he came to me, no matter what form he took.

I cleared my throat. "We go to the terralings then, and we get the information we need."

He nodded. "At all costs."

Oka pressed against me. "For Frost."

I held a hand out to King and he set his palm against mine. It was as familiar to me as if I'd held him a hundred times. "Are they still near the redwoods?" I asked.

"Yes, they managed to keep their trees." He laughed.

I thought about the redwoods, the last place I'd known the terralings to live. The massive trunks, the underbrush, the feeling of safety that had always been there, and wove spirit through the three of us. The mountain lake was gone in a blink and then we were standing amongst trees that were hundreds of years old. They'd not been destroyed in the breaking of the world, which meant we were likely not far from the terralings' home. They would have fought for the earth, for the trees, just like King had said.

But they wouldn't fight for Frost? Or for me when I needed help, when I was being bound away from my magic? My jaw tightened and I held onto the sudden burst of anger, an emotion that had seen me through so much.

"This way," King said softly. "The day is shortening and we need to slip through under the shadow of night if we are going to go in quietly."

I glanced at Oka. "You ready to do some spying?"

She gave me a wide tiger grin, showing off her massive canines. "Not like this I suppose?"

I shook my head and she shifted to her house cat form. In a blink, she shot ahead of us, leaping through the bushes and thick ferns, over fallen logs and then on farther until I couldn't see her any longer. King glanced at me, worry on his face.

"She won't be captured?"

"Raven knows who she is, but what are the chances he's here? He's likely looking for me, so I can't believe he'd actually think I'd come here," I said. "I doubt anyone else will make the connection between her and me."

He nodded. "You are not what I expected."

That caught me by surprise. Was it because of Mac's influence on him? "What do you mean? How could you expect me at all?"

He held a low-hanging branch up for me to walk under. "You don't know about the prophecies that involve an elemental witch?"

"No." I shook my head. "And I'm not sure I want to either." Prophecies had always found a way of turning out badly. Like Liam's death. Like losing Alex. Like Lark destroying the world. "I am done with them. I rule me; no more prophecies, no more stories of what could be or might be. They are beyond cruel to offer hope amidst so much hurt."

"You believe that?" he asked. "That they are meant to do harm?"

I thought about his question a moment, really looking at all I'd seen in my life so far when it came to prophecies before I spoke, my words growing more certain with each step.

"How could they not? Look at this world, destroyed because Lark followed a prophecy and I helped her do it. It is the perfect example of the stupidity of following the words of people long dead, or of seers who can't interpret what they see. It's not like they turn out well. Not one of them. Even though the world is saved, how many people had their lives taken, or completely destroyed? I cannot believe now that I am older, and not so naïve, that there was not a better way." I pulled one of my knives and sliced it across the tops of a few ferns. "Have you had any prophecies about you?"

He laughed. "A few."

"You won't tell me?"

Like me, he was thoughtful a moment before answering. "Perhaps I like what you said about them not being able to control us. To stop them and the grief they bring. Though there is one I wouldn't mind coming to light. One of flesh and bodies." He shot me a grin that curled my toes, the mixture of love for Mac and a desire to hold him tight. To feel his heart beat again against mine.

I swallowed and took a cleansing breath. "Something about me, I assume?"

He nodded. "Yes, but I will let that play out as it wants to as well. You have suffered, and lost, and been broken. I'm not going to add to that."

That had Mac written all over it. That understanding that I would be ready when I was ready.

"Thank you," I said softly. He bobbed his head and I thought about how the Mother Goddess had brought Mac back to me. How she'd known how much I needed him. I couldn't help but be grateful, even if his reappearance was somewhat unconventional.

The forest leaned in around us, and for a moment, I thought I felt the Mother Goddess, felt her presence under my feet and all around me. But it was fleeting and gone before I could truly hang onto it.

"The truth, Pamela—"

"No, don't call me that." I stopped him, feeling a strange rush flow over me.

"That's your name, isn't it?" He raised an eyebrow.

It was my name, and it wasn't. Not anymore. Something in me was changing and I had to find a way to find my feet. I wanted to drop a hand on Oka, to feel her approval of what I was going to say. But for the first time in forever, I didn't worry that she would leave me. That I would scare her away. "My mother named me Thorn. I think . . . I think I will go by that now."

He shot a look at me. "An elemental's name? Are you

sure you want that, knowing how we can be? Knowing the legacy of that bloodline?"

"No, not an elemental name, but the name my mother gave me," I said, thinking of my mother. Of how she'd loved me. "She died trying to protect me from the prophecies written about me, about the potential in me that could be darkened and warped. I . . . I think it's time I honored her for that."

King nodded. "I think that is wise, and fitting."

A rush of warmth cascaded through me with his approval, and I had to work to push it away. "Does that kind of flattery work for you?"

A laugh escaped him, but he caught it quickly and smothered it with a hand. "Sometimes. Usually. But not with you, I think?" His smile was genuine, sweet, and it took everything in me to hold my hands to myself. He was right, we needed to let this play out however it would. I could wait to have Mac back in my life. I could hang on a little longer.

I shook my head. "I value strength, loyalty, and someone who won't die on me. Someone who will do all he must to survive, to not leave my side."

He stopped moving, turned and caught one of my hands. "I'm a survivor, above all else. I won't die easily. I won't give up no matter what the cost of living is."

I gave his hand a squeeze, then let him go. Too easy, it would be too easy to let my bruised and battered heart let this one in. I had to hold him off, at least a little.

If for nothing else, for Sam's warning. That he was dangerous.

And because I could see the reflection of myself in his

dark eyes. I could see the tears between light and dark and the realization that not everyone would understand the choices I was going to make.

A rustle in the bushes slowed my feet and I dropped to a crouch, King beside me.

A blur of orange leapt out of the bushes and landed in front of me. "You aren't going to believe it, but Raven is *here.*"

I dug my hands into the soil in front of me, anxiety crashing over me. He was going to be angry, and I wasn't sure just how to handle an angry Raven. But there was a chance I could make it in without being seen. "He had his power inside your skull." I looked at King. "You need to stay out here. I'll go in and get the information."

He nodded. "And if you get into trouble? How will I know?"

"I'll light a flare," I said, feeling my connection to fire under my skin heat and whisper of the destruction it could do with this forest. Ripe for the plucking, I could burn it down, force Belladonna to tell me where Frost was. I put a hand to my head, banishing those dark thoughts. That was not me. I would never do that. "I can use my cloak. They won't even see me."

Oka climbed onto my shoulder and I pulled the hood of my cloak up as I wove spirit through it. King blinked a few times, staring at me. "Amazing, you just disappeared. You are still there?"

I smiled, and reached out and brushed my fingers against his chin. He grinned back, an answering pulse of the ocean's power rumbling along my skin, a whisper of the Arctic cold and the rumble of a bear I knew to the depths of my soul. Power, he was power and that was safety. That was what I'd been looking for.

Not a sheep in wolf's clothing.

A true power to be reckoned with. One that wouldn't die on me. Or push me away because of my strength.

I pushed through the bushes, keeping my eyes on the terrain, watching for any terralings that might be on guard. Forcing myself to move before I did something I would regret later.

"Like kiss him?" Oka laughed softly. "I cannot understand it, but it would not be wrong. At least that is the impression I get."

"He has Mac's soul inside him," I said.

She shook her head. "I know, you showed me that, but how is that possible?"

"The Mother Goddess gave him a second chance. I don't know why she used the undine king's body, but he is there, inside him. Loving me still."

Oka's confusion came through loud and clear. "I've never heard of such a thing, but then there is much with you that is new to me. The Mother Goddess knows what she is doing."

I agreed with her. The Mother Goddess had never been wrong before. She'd led me to Oka years ago, and now Mac was back in my life.

"I just have to be patient," I said. "I can do that."

Oka laughed softly. "Really? You almost kissed him back there."

I smiled and then hurried my pace. "You stay out of it."

We needed to focus. Slipping into the terralings' home

was no small thing. There would be guards, and if Raven was there, he might have set them against me.

Truth.

I steeled myself for what I was about to do. I needed to find Belladonna as quickly as I could and get into her head. She would give me the location of the sylphs' home, one way or another.

I was done fucking around with these elementals. They would either get out of my way, or they would die. I would make them rue the day they crossed me, the day they took Frost and threatened Rylee.

Oka pressed her head against mine and a flicker of energy danced through her and into me, an energy I felt reflected in my own soul. "Enough pandering to them, I agree. They will pay for what they've done. There will be no other way with them. They are all too filled with pride to see the damage they've done."

I lifted a hand to her head. She was my soul; she was the one I could always depend on. And maybe King now too.

He was what I needed. He was the one I'd been waiting for.

And Mac would be back in my arms soon enough.

We slipped through the trees, Oka and I, silently, working our way toward the terralings' village. Toward where Belladonna waited, her head full of the information I needed. I tried to still the anxiety that cut through me, reminding me that Bella was not a bad person, and that I was about to take information by force from her.

"There's no other way," Oka said. "You have to do it. You think she'll offer the information willingly?"

Oka was not wrong, but I didn't like it. This was one of those decisions that I'd known would come. Where others would look at what I did as something bad, and I looked at it as necessary. I steeled myself as we drew closer to the village.

"Let me go in first again." Oka jumped from my shoulder and appeared in front of me as if out of thin air. "Then follow at a distance."

She trotted out of the cover of the trees and bush, and down the long stretch of hard-packed earth. I watched her go a minute, her body visible even in the dark of the early evening. Pale orange was not what I would call camouflage.

She flicked her tail up and showed me her butt, and I grinned at her sass. I gave her another ten seconds and then I stepped out of the cover of the trees. Yes, my cloak was keeping me invisible, a trick I'd learned from Raven years ago, but that didn't mean I couldn't be detected.

Elementals were powerful and cagey at the best of times. Seeing as right now they were trying to kill me and I was walking right into one of their dens, this was about as dangerous as I could get in that moment.

But for Frost, for Rylee, I would do it a thousand times over. I just hated that I knew what they would think of me, that they would believe me to be like Raven was in his youth, stirring up trouble for the sake of trouble, not seeing that what I was doing was protecting those I loved.

A tear caught me off guard, at the tip of my eyelashes. I dashed it away and hurried to catch up to Oka.

She approached the side of a massive willow tree that was far beyond what any natural willow tree would be. The top of it competed with the redwoods around us. My first thought was that it was stunning, a true beauty, and of course, that would be where Bella would set up her throne room.

Oka tucked in beside the willow tree, away from the guards, her ears swiveling.

I couldn't ask her what she was hearing or what was happening.

And a split second later, it didn't matter. A hand shot through the willow branches and clamped down on her neck and dragged her through. Her fear shot through me like an arrow straight through my heart.

"NO!" I screamed the word and lifted my hands, throwing back my cloak. The two guards startled and I threw them out of the way, and forced a wind to whip up, driving the long fronds of the willow tree into the air.

Within its confines was a scene I could not understand at first. Alex stood there, his golden eyes flashing as he held Oka around her neck.

"Make a move, and I'll kill her," he said.

"No, don't hurt her!" I held a hand out, shaking. "Alex, you love her. Don't . . . that's the incubus in you talking, not you."

To the left stood my father, his eyes narrowed. "You need to stop this, Pam."

"Stop what? Bella knows where Frost is. You need to ask her. I'll go with you then, but you need to ask her."

Bella, her long brown hair waving in the wind I still clung to, shook her head. "I don't know where the child is."

Anger and frustration spilled up through me and out my eyes. "You do. I know you do, and you will tell me or I will make you tell me." I drove spirit into her, and her body jerked forward, her eyes blank. Through her mind, I filtered memories, going straight for where Frost was.

"Are you threatening the queen of the terralings?" Raven pointed a finger at me, and I dodged a blast of fire that missed me by inches, lighting up the tree behind me. "She is my sister, and I trust her. Let her go!"

"Well, you shouldn't!" I yelled at him, my eyes continually darting back to Alex and Oka. "Please, don't hurt her.

Alex, this isn't you. You aren't like this. The incubus . . . your father's magic is doing this to you."

"You need to listen to Raven." Alex's eyes were hard and yet they still drew me like a moth to the flame. "You need to do as you're told. You need to submit to the darkness, Pam. Just like I did."

This was insanity! I couldn't believe what I was hearing from either of them. The only thing that made sense was that there was another spirit user, one who'd taken control of them both. I wanted to whip my head around, to look for the source of who was controlling them. I couldn't believe they would both turn on me like this, because I wouldn't do as they wanted.

"Let her go," I whispered, unable to look away from Alex and Oka. "Please, just let her go. Don't hurt her."

Alex arched a brow, haughty and cruel. That was his father's face. I knew it well, and my heart shattered as he tightened his hand around Oka's neck. She thrashed and hissed and I screamed as I threw a bolt of my magic at him, flipping him end over end. I felt her life pull away from me, felt her struggle to breathe. I struggled with her, fighting for her with every ounce of my energy. How could Alex have done this?

He sat up and she was limp in his hands. Limp. Dead. Gone.

He'd snapped her neck. Killed my sweet Oka. I reached for the bond between us but it was torn, shredded in death. I couldn't feel her at all. This wasn't happening, it couldn't be! Pain tore through me as if it were my neck broken alongside hers.

"NO!" The scream ripped out of me and the world

blurred. I wanted to thrash them all, kill them for this. I wanted to scoop Oka up and run away with her, to heal her. Because for her, I would have given up all the others. I would have walked away from Frost even, as terrible and evil as that might have made me, it was the truth. She was my soul.

And she'd been killed right in front of me by my best friend.

"Not evil," Mac whispered as he dragged me away, "You are not evil, my girl. You love fiercely and with every part of your heart. You can't save her though; she's gone. Gone. And we have to go too."

He helped me turn and bolt away from the redwood village, half carrying me as I sobbed until we were outside the edge of the protection of the village.

As soon as we were clear, I jumped us through the Veil with a simple weave of spirit, dragging Mac with me. I fell out of the Veil to my hands and knees, my whole body shaking.

Oka was dead.

Alex had killed her. He was overcome with his incubus powers.

I couldn't un-see his hand around her neck, the limp hang of her tiny body. I tipped my head back and howled like a wounded animal, pain and rage mixing with my magic and spilling out around me, suffusing the plants and earth, the wind and rocks. The world shook, and I didn't know if it was me, or if it was the actual ground shaking.

I didn't care, not with Oka dead. My soulmate was dead and it was all *my fault*. I never should have sent her in. I never should have let her go without me. "My fault, it's my fault."

Someone was yelling my name, over and over. "Thorn, stop it! You're going to kill us!"

A sharp slap whipped my head to the side, stunning me, literally snapping me out of the maelstrom raging in my head and through my heart.

King crouched in front of me. "They will pay for this, but if you keep up with this, you'll kill us both. Your familiar wouldn't want you to die. Would she?"

The tremors rocketing through me slowed, and I looked around. The ground was cracked, trees had been torn from their roots and several fires dotted the land. It looked like the world had been right after the rending. I put a hand to my forehead. "He killed her. I can't feel her at all." I put a fist to my mouth, my teeth against my knuckles as I tried to make sense of what I'd seen.

Alex had done this? Could it have been someone else, someone impersonating him? Because to think he would snap Oka's neck, I just couldn't believe it even though I'd seen it happen. I'd felt her die.

King tugged me into his arms, and I fell against him, sobbing. What was happening? Why would Alex have killed Oka?

"I thought he loved her too," I whispered. But then the scene from the dream world came back to me. How we'd been so close, our bodies pressed against one another, and Oka had been the one to pull as apart. To push him away and say that he wasn't safe. Hadn't she? I put a hand to my head, trying to make sense of my memories. Oka had pushed Alex away, hadn't she?

Truth.

I frowned, hiccupping sobs escaping me. Could he have killed her out of retribution for keeping him from fucking me? Or if I had turned him down . . . this would be a way of getting back at me. I couldn't believe that he would do that, that he could be so petty and cruel. Not if he cared for me, not knowing the bond I had with my cat. I pressed my face against King's chest, breathing in the combination of salty water and Arctic cold.

If that was the truth, as I felt in my bones, then there was only one answer. The incubus in Alex had fully taken over and my friend, the man I loved, was gone. The next time I saw him, I had to see him as an enemy. There would be no other choice if I wanted to survive. The tears didn't stop as my thoughts darkened. Even though he'd killed Oka, I didn't want to kill him. I didn't want to lose him too.

You've already lost him. I nodded, knowing Sam was right. I had already lost him.

"He killed her," I whispered. "I just can't believe it."

"He did." He stroked my hair. "Why did he kill her?"

"Revenge. I didn't . . . he wanted to be with me."

King's arms tightened around me. "You turned him down, and he killed your familiar. Then he will come for me next."

My head snapped up, horror flashing through me. I was a fool, and King was right. Because he carried Mac's soul, and Alex had been in competition with Mac from the very beginning. "No, I won't let him hurt you. I refuse to let him take you from me too."

He smiled down at me, Mac's face superimposed over

King's. "You might not feel it yet, but you were meant to free me, Thorn. You were meant to stand at my side. The power of the elements between us will be enough to change the world. To show the elementals that they cannot bind power away from those who have it." His hand tangled in the hair at the back of my head and he pulled me close, his lips crushing over mine.

And all I could think was that this was Mac. Mac was kissing me. I wrapped my arms around him, holding him tightly to me. I might have lost Oka, and as horrendous as that was, I had a second chance with Mac. I wouldn't take it for granted. I wasn't going to let one moment of it pass without drinking him in to the fullest.

My arms circled up around his neck and I tugged him close, silencing any lingering doubts that maybe this was too soon. Maybe I should let my heart heal from losing Oka. But the truth was, we could die tomorrow. I refused to regret again, to wish I'd loved him more. To wish I had given him all of me.

I could lose him. I'd waited too long for Mac the first time, and then waited for Alex and lost them both—one to death, and one to the darkness. My mind and body disconnected as he—Mac—pulled my clothes off and I did the same to him until that frantic hunger for being touched eased. I'd never had sex before, and to have my first with someone I thought I'd lost was beyond special, it was everything to me. Everything.

I wanted—no, needed—to feel a connection to someone, to something bigger than myself, and his ocean-kissed skin was everything in those moments. He was my Mac, my bear, my world. He was my love and my reason for not giving up, for not burying myself along-side Oka.

He spoke to me of love, of fate, of being everything I would ever need. That he would never leave my side, that he was stronger now. His teeth bit into me, marking me as his.

Beware the bite of the bear.

King's dark eyes never left my face and I wondered if he really believed that he loved me after just a few hours. He didn't know that what he was feeling was Mac's connection to me. I felt a little bad, about that. About King not realizing that it wasn't him I wanted, but the soul he housed.

"I am your Romeo," he whispered, holding my naked body to his, skin still slick with sweat and his eyes at half-mast, glazed with desire still. I sat up and pulled away from him, suddenly cold.

"That story doesn't end well for Romeo," I pointed out, pulling my clothing back on. The grief over Oka was not gone, but it was fading, easing the longer she was away from me. That was good. I had to go on. I had to find Frost. I couldn't grieve. Just like I couldn't grieve Mac. Like I couldn't grieve Alex and what he'd become.

No, Alex would die. I'd kill him myself if I had to, to stop him from hurting anyone else. My throat tightened at the thought of him dying in my arms, like Mac. I pressed the heels of my hands into my eyes and made myself breathe through the panic that slid over me, the rush of anxiety so strong, I wasn't sure I could get my next breath.

"It is a profound love story," King said. I glanced at

him as he sat up and leaned forward. His body was rock solid, muscles in all the right places. He rubbed a hand over his chest and winked at me as if he'd caught me drooling.

I rolled my eyes. "Please, Romeo and Juliet were fools. They died when they could have lived. They died when they should have fought harder to survive."

"They were fated to be together," he said. "Even in death, their love was strong. That is all I meant."

I could feel his hurt as I could feel Mac's when he'd been alive. I reached over and brushed a hand across his jaw line, thinking that Mac had indeed come back to me in death, so perhaps I should go a little easier on King. "So, I am your Juliet, the one fated to be at your side?" I made myself smile, even though my heart raced and my body wanted nothing more than to run, to move.

His hand cupped my one calf and he tried to tug me back to the ground to him. "You are. No elemental has ever consumed my mind and body like you. It is like I have known you longer than this last day. I don't understand it, but I feel it."

Mac. Goddess, he was feeling Mac's emotions—that was the only explanation. "I feel it too. But you will understand when I say we have to keep moving," I said softly. I bent and put a hand under his chin. "You will understand that we need to find Frost, above all else. He is the key to stopping the elementals."

His smile was slow and he pulled my fingers away from his chin to nip at them. "For you, my love, my witch, my Thorn, I will follow anywhere you go. Consider me your slave."

"No," I whispered, shaking my head as I took a step back. "Never that. Love me, but don't ever bow to me."

I bent and gathered up his clothes, and tossed them to him, suddenly needing some space between us. "Unless you plan to go to the sylphs' home naked, I suggest you put your clothing back on."

He did as I asked him to, but a frown creased his handsome face. "But we did not find out where the sylphs are hiding. Did we?"

"The broken mountains," I said, still seeing the place in my mind, the place I'd taken from Belladonna while Alex had held Oka.

"Yes, but that range is massive, running nearly the length of the world now."

I didn't know that, but it didn't matter. "I was in Belladonna's head, remember? And I paid the price to get that knowledge." I'd let Oka die.

I heaved where I stood, the series of events too much. I'd let her die to get the information I'd needed! Oh, goddess, why did I not see that before? I'd let Alex hold her while I took what I needed, and she'd died because of it—

"Shh, shhh, that's not true! He killed her for the pleasure of it. That's what an incubus does. They suck life away. It wouldn't have mattered what you'd done, Thorn. It wouldn't." King was holding me again, rocking me gently. I pushed him away.

"I don't deserve comfort." I wanted to scream my grief, to cry for hours and sink into the pain that kept pulsing through me. But then I would lose Frost too. If I lost him, and the elementals went for Rylee . . . my body heaved again, fighting everything I felt.

King stood and finished tucking his shirt into his pants. "Then should we go?"

I nodded and closed my eyes, imagining the eastern slopes of the broken mountains. I wasn't limited in jumping to only places I'd been to, but still it had been a long time since I'd had to choose a place I'd not visited.

"After the boy, what then?" King asked softly, his hands sliding around my body. Hugging my back to his front. I sighed and put a hand over his, once more letting him take my weight. How many times had Mac carried me? Taken my weight and let me rest? Too many. And he was here again, holding me up.

"I need to go home. To deal with one last thing. The elementals threatened my family. I saw them." I spoke the words and fear jagged through me like a lightning bolt. We had to move, we had to hurry. There were only three days, and we were through one already and hadn't found Frost yet.

I lifted one hand and pressed it to my eyes. "We have to hurry."

"We have time, the elementals are not looking for us now." He kissed my shoulder and began to pull my clothes off again. "They would have found us by now if they were looking. You put a scare into them back there, we both did."

"No, we have to go, we have to go now!" I struggled in his arms, but he turned me around as if I were a child.

Panic set my heart to thumping painfully in my chest and my eyes pooled up with tears until they overflowed and ran down my cheeks. Where was Oka when I needed her to back me up? Dead, because of my stupidity. My pride. "You don't understand, there is a time limit."

"Don't cry, don't cry," King whispered, kissing the tears away. "I won't leave you, I swear it. And there is no time limit."

I brought my arms up and knocked him off me. "No, stop it. No more. I need to go. Are you coming with me or not?"

Anger replaced the panic, hot and with a cleansing burn that I welcomed. Because it wasn't his leaving that had me terrified. It was the feelings, or lack thereof, that should have been inside of me. Where was the pain from losing Oka? Thinking of her should have had me in a mess again, but I barely felt anything now that she was gone.

"Too much hurt, and we begin to shut it all off," King said. "I know that. The undines killed my familiar too, Thorn. They killed him and he was my best friend. You've been through too much. Later, when things are not so hard, so dangerous, you will grieve then. Your heart and mind are in a protective mode, keeping you moving so you can do what you must."

I blinked rapidly but couldn't stop the tears. "And that's why I slept with you?"

He smiled and sighed. "No, I think even through the chaos of this moment your heart and soul recognize me for who I am to you."

But was he? Was he the one I'd waited for? Hadn't I waited for Alex for years? He was Mac, I knew that much, so that had to be it.

A rush of cold flowed up and through me, calming, putting out the fires of fear that had cropped up inside me. "You're right. Later, I will grieve those I love later."

"Good girl. Let's go get that boy then, yes?" He held his hand out to me, dashing and dangerous, so full of power and with Mac's soul. How could he be wrong?

I nodded, meshed my fingers with his and wove spirit through us, taking us away from the crystalline lake to the eastern slope of the broken mountains. The world blinked and wobbled and for just a moment I thought I heard laughter.

Was that King laughing?

No, it had been a woman's voice, I was sure of it. I blinked and took in our new destination, the sound of laughter fading.

My feet sank into the soft, powdery snow. It fell from the sky and blew around us, the icy crystals scattering across my still-damp cheeks. They crusted up, pulling at my skin.

"Sweet dark goddess, this is too cold!" King barked the words, his teeth already chattering. I sighed and wove a thin line of fire through his clothes, binding it with a combination of spirit and my blood magic. Too bad he wasn't fully Mac yet. He'd be able to handle this cold better.

His eyes widened and he patted a hand over his skin. "How did you do that?"

I winked at him. "Magic."

A laugh rippled out of him and he took my hand and pulled me to him for a quick kiss. I breathed him in, the ocean and the fresh clean tang of the water we were so far from. Now, all I had to do was find Frost, take him with me, and then deal with one last obstacle. Then I could go and grieve.

Then I could take the stopgap out of my emotions and I could let them bleed out all around me for the first time in what felt like forever.

I closed my eyes and did a slow turn, letting his fingers go.

"What are you—"

"Hush," I said. "Tracking an elemental is no easy task."

Tracking an elemental, is that what I was doing? No, more than that. I was tracking Raven. He would come here. I was sure of it. *No, no, you aren't a Tracker. You shouldn't be able to do this. This is a dark magic, deeper than anything of yours!* Sam's voice was barely heard above the blowing of the wind, and to be fair I ignored her. I didn't need her right now.

Because it wasn't Raven's energy that I found waiting nearby.

No, I found Alex's energy.

My eyes flew open and before King could grab me, I leapt away from him, using spirit to cover the short distance between me and Alex.

He'd killed Oka, snapped her neck as if she were nothing. Shattered my bond to her. Stolen what was left of my soul.

I'd make him rue the day he ever laid hands on her.

ALEX

There was nothing to do but push the caravan on and hope that we got clear of the elementals that were hounding us now that we were out of the flooded ravine. Wade said they were still back there, still watching us, but keeping their distance.

Apparently I'd given them enough of a scare they were going to give us a wide berth, for now at least.

Richard didn't say much, allowing me to drive the caravan for the day, then allowing me to set up the watch guard, along with who would hunt and who would stay close to the caravan.

Wade walked beside me as we scouted the next day's path that evening. On four legs I could cover ground quickly, and Wade being an elemental easily kept up—he said it was his connection to the earth that allowed him to do that.

"Should we turn back?" he asked as we loped along. We were close to where we would turn around and head back to the caravan. Ahead of us the terrain changed suddenly from the mostly flat plains of the caravan to something more, something I didn't think I'd ever see again. Something that made me remember Peta's words.

Huge redwood trees shot up into the sky, reaching for the clouds as if they'd not been touched during the breaking of the world.

"This is impossible," Wade said. "This is the . . . this is impossible." He did a slow turn and looked behind us, as if that direction would give him the answer he needed.

I shifted to two legs, clothes and all. Yeah, I really should have learned that a long time ago. "What is impossible about this? Did you expect something else? We've been looking at this dark line of something for the last couple of hours. Why do trees shock you?"

"Because it's not that it's trees, but . . . this is the home of the terralings. I can feel it under my skin, but I thought that the last few hours I was imagining things. That I wasn't feeling this, but just a memory of it because I was missing my home. I left the redwoods as the world was breaking, I made a run for it. But to find it here . . . I don't know what to make of it." Wade's hand shook as he ran it over his face.

"Do we need to go around?" I asked.

This was where I was supposed to leave the caravan, but that didn't mean I wouldn't try to see them as far as I could.

"Terralings shouldn't bother the caravan, but they might try to force me to stay." He said softly, "I don't know. I left before I could truly see if Belladonna was going to be a monster of a queen like her father was."

I nodded, feeling a pull toward those trees. "I'll go in as a wolf, see what I can see. You head back to the caravan and get them ready to move. Just in case."

Wade nodded and didn't argue. Not that I was surprised. He wasn't the arguing kind. I shifted back to four legs and jogged toward the trees, scenting the air as I went. The night was just starting to fall, the sky dusky, and that set the trees under an early cover of darkness. That would work in my favor with my black, silver-tipped fur. On the gentle breeze there was nothing but the smell of a forest, the undergrowth, small animals, and hint of water like a stream.

But the second I stepped under the cover of the trees, a ripple of energy slid over my body. Like someone already knew I was there. I didn't slow, just kept on moving as if I were just a lone wolf going for a wander, finding the paths of the forest that took me deeper and deeper. A whiff of something caught my nose, Pamela's scent, and for just a second, I thought I saw a flash of orange ahead of me.

Was this why I was supposed to leave the caravan? To meet up with Pamela and Oka and go with them?

I hurried my pace but there were no more flashes of orange, no more whiffs of Pam's unique smell.

The trees around me loomed, but I ignored them, following the tiny bits of scent I did pick up. The smell of sweat, of leather, of elementals, of campfires and cooking food. The forest thickened heavily and I thought I wouldn't be able to get through the tangle of brambles, trees and bush, but at the last second a path opened up.

I jogged down it and into a clearing, past a guard who

nodded at me as if he knew me. He didn't, of course, but maybe he thought I was just a regular wolf. Possible. Maybe he even thought I was a familiar.

Swiveling my ears, I picked up on a voice I knew.

Raven.

My jog turned into a flat-out sprint, forgetting that I was supposed to be figuring out if we could get the caravan through here. Where Raven was, Pam was. It had to have been Oka I saw earlier, had to have been Pam I'd smelled and not just my imagination creating what I wanted. But why hadn't I felt Oka through our bond?

What had happened in the short time we'd been apart?

With my Alpha senses, I reached for Oka, and found her behind me but drawing closer. I could wait for her or go to Raven.

Raven yelled something, fury in his words, and I scooted forward, my decision made.

The terralings' home was similar to the one I'd known before, with homes set up around a long narrow oval. Smoke curled up out of those homes, lights in the windows, a few people still outside. Normal, this all looked normal. I turned my head and Raven's smell filled my nose. I followed it to the largest non-redwood tree in the village.

Ahead of me a large willow tree rose almost as high as the redwoods, the long fronds of the tree sweeping across the dusty, hard-packed ground. Two guards stood on either side of what I supposed was the entrance. They saw me coming and I braced myself for a fight.

"Griffin," one said, and pulled open the long tree

branches for me. Griffin? They thought I was *that* old wolf? I shook my head, didn't matter. I'd use it to my advantage. I nodded my head at them, keeping my mouth shut, and slid through the opening they offered me.

Under the cover of the willow tree, the scene was something else from the quiet of the elementals' village. Raven stood toe to toe with his sister, Belladonna.

"I will not hunt my own daughter!"

"She is losing herself and you know it!" Belladonna slapped her hands on the table beside her. "This is outside any prophecy, Raven. Something has changed, and she is letting the darkness take her. She is embracing it even! We cannot allow it! The damage she can do is beyond measure, beyond anything we've seen before!"

"I will not hunt her!" He roared the words, his voice cracking with emotion. "She can be saved, Bella, she has to be! I can't lose her too!"

Belladonna looked to me and her eyes softened, sadness warring with determination. "Griffin, thank the gods you are here. Please, talk to him, please."

I shifted to two legs and she gasped. Raven spun and his eyes narrowed. "How did you find this place?"

"It's in the path of the caravan," I said. "And Peta told me I'd leave the caravan once I reached the trees. What happened to Pam? Why would you want to hunt her?"

Raven sighed and his head dropped until his chin touched his chest. "Something happened to her when she fought the First Witch. I'm not sure what but . . . she is not herself. I've felt it both times I've healed her body. And I'm not sure she even knows."

I thought about our encounter in the dream world, about the intimacy and then how she'd acted like nothing had happened. I wanted to tell them they were wrong, that she was fine. But I knew they were not wrong.

I told them briefly of our encounter, leaving out the more intimate details. "She was . . . it was like she didn't see what was happening as it was happening. She thought I'd attacked her, that I'd tried to drain her power, but that wasn't the case. She pushed me away."

Raven shook his head. "If the First Witch has a hold on her, then . . . she may not be seeing anything as it truly is, but being fed a perception that makes her do as the First Witch wants."

"I love her, but I don't . . . I don't know if that is enough." I looked at Raven and his eyes narrowed.

"You slept with her, didn't you?"

I lifted my hands above my head. "I thought I was dreaming, Raven. It wasn't until after . . . it was after that she seemed more herself. But then she thought I'd attacked her."

Raven took a big breath. "Listen to me. The First Witch likely tried to influence you. But you're an incubus; that is a hard creature to influence on a good day, never mind when you are operating from a space of love."

"There's a point to you telling me this?" I was trying not to freak out that I'd basically had sex with the First Witch, not Pamela at all. That it had been without her even being aware, that she didn't know. I had never loved someone more, and to know I'd done something without her consent tore me up inside.

"Because it means that her familiar will be under the

same spell, and will be helping keep the delusion up." Raven shook his head.

Belladonna closed her eyes and put a hand to her chest. "The power in her will eventually eat away the love she has for those in her life until there is nothing left."

I thought about Oka, about their bond. "And her cat?"

"She will darken with her."

"Can that perception be broken, do you think?" My mind was racing, working through the problem, fighting to find a way through it. "Oka is the one soul who could get through to her, they are connected deeper than any others." I paced a small circle, an idea forming. "What if I could snap Oka away from her? Then we could use Oka to reach Pam."

Raven stared at me. "You think you can untangle a familiar from their charge? Those bonds are legendary for a reason, Alex."

I think that was the first time he'd used my name.

I thought about the bond between Oka and me, about the fact that she was part of my pack. Different than what she had with Pam, but still, I could see where I could make an inroad with her. I nodded slowly. "She's part of my pack. I'm her Alpha, so she has to obey me. It's part of the package there. And while it's not a guarantee, it's worth trying." I almost said *seeing as they are here*, but I bit the words back.

A look between Belladonna and Raven was weighted with possibilities. "These things happen for a reason," she said softly. "We cannot let her reach the boy. Not with this darkness on her. She would warp him to become her protégé. He will be strong, Raven, so very strong. He could be the leader we've been waiting for if guided the right way. The other elementals were right to take him away."

"They were not right!" Raven snapped. "I could have protected him. He's my son. And they should have told me what they were doing."

Belladonna leaned on the table. "I *know* they should have, Raven. You have given them enough reasons not to be trusted in the past, and now so has your daughter. Even now, I do not know how far to trust you." She paused and locked eyes with him. "But we are beyond all of that and must deal with the monster we've created. If this wolf thinks he has a way to bring Pamela back from the brink, then I say we let him try. There is nothing else we've got at this point, no signposts, no directions."

Raven looked like he was torn between throwing up and throwing a fit. The seconds passed as I stood watching him. Waiting him out. Listening to the sounds around us and waiting for Oka and Pam to show themselves. They were close.

"If they are together, she will fight for her cat," he said softly, his eyes tired. "I can hold Pamela at bay," his voice cracked and he swallowed hard. "Goddess help me, I will hold her at bay while you break their bond, or whatever it is you think you can do."

Belladonna's eyes filled with tears. "I am sorry, brother. I truly am. This was not what any of us wanted."

They spoke like Pamela was already gone, but they didn't know her. Whatever was going on, I knew she could be brought back. "She has more heart in her than you are giving her credit for," I said. "More fight than you know, than you've ever seen."

That was her, that was who she was, and the strength in her was more than anyone else I knew—with one exception. Rylee.

A soft sound at the doorway caught my ears. I held up a finger and they went quiet. I turned and went to the edge of the willow tree's branches and stood there, listening, smelling.

On the other side, Oka was doing the same, by the smell of it.

I went to a crouch and closed my eyes, feeling the bond between us, feeling how tenuous it was. "Oka."

Just her name and I felt her pause, felt the bond between us waver. That was not going to happen. "Pam's in trouble, Oka. I need you here with me, so we can bring her back. You can't save her on your own, not this time. I need you to be the strong one this time."

If I could touch her, the bond would be strengthened. A low hiss rolled out of her and I did the only thing I could. I shot a hand through the long branches and grabbed her by the scruff. She twisted and her skin shivered under my hand as she started to shift into her tiger form as I dragged her through.

"No, do not shift!" I bellowed the words as I pulled her in with me, pushing all the power of an Alpha into my voice.

Huge pale green eyes stared up at me as she whimpered. "You are not my boss."

"I am," I said, softer this time as I brought her carefully to my chest. "Oka, stay with me here. You are the only hope we have of stopping her. You will be the deciding factor. You are the best of her, Oka." I tried to block her from Pamela, to push my bond to a point of overcoming the one with Pamela.

Her eyelids fluttered and tears leaked into her fur. "Don't do this! I can't leave her!"

The wind outside picked up and the tree rattled around us. Raven strode forward just as the branches were all flung upward, suspended as if the tree had been turned upside down. I hung onto Oka and stared at Pamela. Her cloak was up over her head, and her hair hung forward, whipping around with the blast of wind she'd created.

"Let my cat go." Her voice was hard, full of ice and anger. "Or I will kill you where you stand."

I pressed Oka to my chest, hanging not only onto her physically, but to the bond between us, tightening it, strengthening it. Maybe it wasn't as strong as what she had with Pamela, but I was banking on Oka being able to see that this was the way to save her girl.

"Oka, something is wrong with her, and if you stay with her now, we won't be able to save her. If you stay with her now, her fate in the darkness will be sealed!"

She hissed and thrashed in my arms, her tiny razor claws slashing across my chest, opening me up as if they were knives. But she didn't shift. She could have at that point, but she didn't. "Knock me out," she whispered as she fought, as if she wanted to be free. "Let her see you knock me out or I will have to go to her."

I didn't know how to knock her out without hurting

her, so I wrapped one hand around her tiny neck and squeezed.

The scream that erupted out of Pamela cut into me worse than Oka's claws, pain and horror woven in one word.

"NO!"

The wind smashed into me, hot and fury-filled, flames erupting everywhere it touched as the two elements were woven together. This was going so wrong, all wrong. As I hit the dirt, I cradled Oka to me, holding her limp body to me. Her heart beat, she was alive, but I'd knocked her out. And with her out, I cut her off from Pamela with one last push, wrapping my bond over top of the one with Pamela, covering it.

And now Pamela thought I'd killed her familiar.

The flames around us rose higher, snapping through the willow tree with a wicked crackle eating up the perfect tinder. Shouts rose as the elementals ran to put the fire out, ran to get the flames doused.

It wouldn't work, though. I lay on my side, Oka with me, and stared at the girl I'd loved for years. Her head was thrown back and her hands were raised as the flames snarled around her, not touching her. A man I didn't recognize strode to her side. Blue hair and black eyes, I was sure he was a water elemental. A flicker, and it was not an undine, but Mac at her side. He looked at me and winked.

Raven pointed a finger at him. "You are not needed here."

If I'd thought the shit had hit the fan before, it was nothing to what happened next. Pamela flung a hand at her father and the coil of power that hit him sent him end over end. The blue-haired man blocked another elemental as one of the guards rushed Pamela.

"Thorn, we must go!" he called to her. Thorn? What the hell?

Confusion rocketed through me.

"No, Belladonna, you will tell me where the boy is. You will tell me now!" Her voice echoed with power and I saw the queen of the terralings step forward as if her own will was overcome.

"Raven!" I spun to see him flat on his back, out cold.

Oka was out cold too.

Which left me.

I tucked Oka against a rock, away from any of the flames, twisted to my feet and shifted to my wolf form.

I shot forward, belly low to the ground and teeth bared. This was not Pamela, this was not my girl. At the last second, she turned to see me and her eyes . . . her eyes were not her own.

I ducked to the side as she flung a hand at me, and I slammed into the legs of her new friend, sending him to the ground with a thud. I shifted back to two legs and grabbed Pam by the arms.

I opened myself to the incubus power in me as the flames raged around us. I didn't want to hurt her. But I didn't know how else to stop her.

"I love you, Pam."

Her eyes closed and she swayed as the power rolled over her. I wanted nothing more than to draw her mouth to mine, to kiss her until she realized that she was loved. Till she realized that she was on a fool's errand. That something was wrong and that I could help her. I would love her no matter what.

Desire flared between us, hot and dark, and nothing like what I'd felt with her before. This was the shadow on her soul opening, and I was drinking it down. She leaned into me for just a second, pressing her cheek against my chest. "I can't fight this, Alex. I'm so sorry."

"No, you have to, you can't give up!"

"Keep her safe," she whispered.

Her eyes flew open and she stared up at me, the words she'd spoken gone in a harsh snarl. "You dare to make me want you when you killed my cat?"

I tried one last pull of power, and felt her energy flow into me, hot and angry. It set my own pulse pounding with a mixture of rage and lust. "This is not you! Fight it!"

She screamed as I tried to drag her energy away. A fist connected with my head and I was thrown backward, and as fast as it had all started, she was gone.

My face throbbed from the blow, but otherwise I wasn't hurt badly. At least not physically. I'd tasted Pam's energy before.

This was not the same. She was stronger, yes, that was true, but she tasted like someone else. She tasted like someone I'd tried to drink down before.

She tasted like the First Witch.

I rolled to the side and puked until my belly was empty, and my body finally gave up the dry heaves. All around me the fires were put out, and people were checked on.

The shouting had died down, and there was a slow-growing fear that Pamela would come back. I made myself move, made myself get to my feet and go to where I'd left Oka. She was still there, and I scooped her up into the crook of my arm. She burrowed in against me, whimpering.

"Pam, my Pam, where has she gone?"

Goddess, what had I done?

13

To say that Raven was a complete mess as the wind and fire from Pamela's attack died down was an understatement. "Goddess, what do we do now? She's teamed up with the worst possible elemental she could have. He's powerful, and without spirit controlling his urges, he's a sociopathic killer!" He strode around the small space of the willow tree throne room, his black cloak flaring out around him. "Damn it, Belladonna, this could have all been avoided if anyone had cared to fill me in!"

I didn't blame him for the anger. I was none too happy either. Oka stirred in my arms. Unhurt physically, but her emotions were all over the map with her connection to Pamela dampened. "Let me get this straight," I said after hearing the full story. "You elementals feared that Pamela would stop you from taking over the world, so you bound her. Then when she broke free, you tried to kill her. Then when that failed, you seemed to recall a prophecy that she was fulfilling and didn't like the direction it was going, so you removed Frost, believing he was in danger from her? And in doing that, you've managed to set her on the worst possible path of the prophecy? Assuming that this prophecy is even about her? You could be making a self-fulfilling prophecy! You could be the ones creating this fucking mess!"

I watched the faces of the undine, sylph and sala-mander representatives who stood near Belladonna and her table. They'd arrived too late to face Pamela, but they were here now. Each one of them slowly nodded.

Oka let out a roaring snarl as she leapt from my arms and landed as a tiger. "You goddess-damned morons! I'm going to lose her because of your fool pride! You've unleashed a monster in her. I could feel it growing and it attached to me. If not for Alex, I would be there still with her!" She bowed her head as sobs and snarls ripped out of her in tandem.

I wasn't sure if she wished she were still with Pam or not, and I knew that was part of the problem. She wanted to be with her charge, with her soul mate. But you can't stay with a soul mate who has lost their way, no matter how much you love them. I knew that, and the truth of it tightened my throat until I couldn't swallow.

I put a hand on her back and she leaned into me. "What do we do, Alex?"

The enormity of the situation was not lost on me. If we couldn't save Pam from herself, then I didn't know what we were going to do. Because the alternative that had been bandied around was not acceptable to me.

To end her. Two people stood at the edge of the group,

their clothing and weapons speaking clearly what they were. The ones who would do the ending.

I tightened my hold on Oka's thick scruff around her neck. "She sees the undine she's with as Mac."

Raven grabbed me by the arm. "What?"

"When they arrived, there was a moment I could see the undine not as he is, but as she sees him. He's Mac to her. Somehow, she believes it."

Oka bowed her head. "That makes sense. She kept saying the Mother Goddess brought him back to her, that she was being given a second chance."

Raven let me go and dropped to a crouch, bowing his head. "The First Witch is doing exactly as I thought. Showing her what her heart wants in a way that allows her to dig in deeply to Pamela's soul. We have to rip that perception away."

"How?" I asked. "How do we do that?"

"There . . . may be a way," Raven said. "But it is dangerous."

"As if she's not dangerous now?" I snapped, then shut my mouth hard, trying to bring my emotions into check. I was still humming with the power I'd drank down, and it made me irritable.

"Oka," I turned to her, "did she say anything else? Did she say what she was going to do, or where she was going if she did find Frost?"

Oka was quiet a moment and I felt the wrestle in her of telling me what Pam planned, and not betraying her charge. Finally she whispered the words, and they were monumental. "She said that the elementals had threatened Rylee. And she would go home after she took care of

Frost. Goddess, do you really think that she would hurt him?"

"She wouldn't, but whoever has a hold of her, I'm not sure," I said.

Raven shook his head. "More than that, the one with her would kill Frost, just for being a potential contestant down the line for power. King is . . . he is worse than his father."

"You're not serious?" I said. "You can't be."

Raven didn't look away from me. "The elemental world is harsh at the best of times, Alex. You've seen it, you've seen the way they have come for Pam. Add to that the inability to stop your natural inclination to kill. She won't be in danger from him, but Frost will." Raven flexed his hand. "I must go to him."

"You can't stop her," Belladonna said. "She's stronger than you, Raven. Her magic is too twisted now, and you do not want to hurt her. You held back, I saw it." The queen looked to the other elementals. "Do not engage her, pull the Enders off her trail. She will kill them without hesitation, I am sure of it."

The other elementals bowed as a unit, though I could see that the ones with the weapons were not happy about it.

I closed my eyes, pain lancing my heart at what I was about to say. "Raven might not be able to stop Pam, but I . . . I know someone who could stop her." I thought. I hoped.

All the eyes in the room turned to me and my stomach rolled. I needed to slow this down. I'd come here looking for passage for the caravan, only to find myself trying to save a child that Pamela had said she'd gone to save. "If anyone can stop her, it would be Rylee."

"The Tracker? She lost her abilities, she's no longer immune to magic," Belladonna said.

"I know, but Pamela was trained to fight by Rylee, and . . . Rylee has faced worse. If anyone can do this, she can. But . . . I think we should look to Frost first. We need a way to keep her from him."

Raven was quiet a moment. "If we go the sylphs' home, I might be able to do something."

We both looked to the white-haired sylph. He sighed and nodded. "We will let you in, Raven. If you think you can protect the child from this danger, we will allow it. This one time."

I nodded. "Do that and then . . . we will wait for her. She will come to us. She is looking for Frost."

"How will she know where to find him?" the sylph asked. "We are well hidden. Not easily found, and very few outside of our own know where we are."

Belladonna lifted her chin, but I saw the gulp of her swallowing. "She was inside my head. She knows where the Eyrie is."

Silence, then the sylph gave a stiff bow. "I must go and warn my queen."

Belladonna waved a hand and the other elementals left her throne room with the exception of Raven. I didn't move and they both turned to me, expectant. "Belladonna, there is something I would ask of you," I said.

She lifted a brow over one perfectly spring-green eye. "Yes?"

"I'm traveling with a caravan of humans and shifters . .

. they are looking for a place called the Haven. Have you heard of it?"

The queen of the earth elementals turned and leaned against a table, then crossed her arms over her ample bosom. "A haven? From what?"

I nodded. "A place where the humans can be safe from this world. From the magic. From all the danger."

Her smile was small and sad, and it twisted a knife in my gut. "There is no such place in this world, Alex. I'm sorry. Perhaps, at one point, the elementals might have been able to help, but we are barely hanging on now. The few humans we have here are protected but—" she held up a hand as I opened my mouth, "we cannot take any more. We will help them, give them supplies and send them on their way. The world is not as dangerous as it was even a few weeks ago. Have you not noticed that?" She opened her mouth as if she'd say something more but closed it quickly.

I wasn't so sure she was right, but I had noticed that there had been no dead land full of shambling zombies, no scarcity of food or water in the last two days. Weird that two days could make you think that things were better. "Thank you. I'll send them through then. And if Wade doesn't want to stay, don't make him."

Both of her eyebrows shot up. "Wade? Do you mean Waderton?"

I smiled. "Is that his full name?"

She nodded. "He left before I fully took power. My father had lost his mind and was not kind to his people. *Wade* is welcome to stay or go as he pleases." She waved me out of her presence and I left, Oka at my side.

She shifted to her smaller form and leapt up into my arms without asking. "Alex, I'm afraid. What if we can't bring her back? What if she's too far gone?"

I sighed and held her tightly, her words echoing my own fears. "I am worried too, Oka. We can't lose her now; we just can't. So we'll fight for her, no matter how hard it gets."

But in my heart of hearts the fear was too deep, a truth I didn't want to look at for what it would show me . . . that we were already too late.

14

PAMELA

I stood in the knee-deep snow, at the base of the sylphs' fortress. I could feel Alex here, but I couldn't see him.

"Alex, you killed Oka. I can't let you get away with that. You have to know that you've gone dark. You've let the incubus take over." *And now I have to stop you. I have to stop the love of my life.*

My hands shook as I turned and I knew exactly why. No matter that he'd done the unthinkable, I wasn't sure I could kill him. I wanted to save him, not hurt him. I did another slow turn and then there was an explosion of snow, and the black-furred wolf I knew so well flew out at me, knocked me down and lay on me.

The warmth of his body soaked right through me, instantaneous and solid. I squeezed my eyes shut and I knew something was so wrong, so terribly wrong.

And it wasn't Alex.

It was me.

Tears crept out from under my squeezed eyelids. "Something's wrong."

"Nothing's wrong. I'm going to tear your fucking throat out." He put his nose under my chin and I held still, wishing I could understand what had become of my world. Nothing was as it should have been, nothing was as it seemed. His cold nose pressed closer and I waited for his teeth.

My mouth moved, I spoke to him, but I couldn't hear my own voice over the buzzing in my ears. His weight grew heavier until I couldn't breathe, and I had to do something or be suffocated. I jammed my hands under him and threw him into the air, spinning to watch him go.

"I'm sorry," I whispered.

"I'm not," he snarled and his incubus magic cascaded over me, drawing me to him, sucking my life force down fast, hard, and with more pleasure than I'd have thought possible.

I stumbled, went to my knees and tried to shake off his hold, but a part of me didn't want to. Part of me wanted to give in to his strength and let him kill me. I'd be with Mac and Oka then. A hand touched my face and I opened my eyes to see him there. Golden eyes I'd thought never to see such anger in, such hatred. How many times had I thought he'd be the one at my side in the end? Not like this though, not like this.

I lashed out, my power striking him in the chest before he could snap my neck and threw him right over the edge of the cliff. His face, the look in his eyes crushed what was left of my heart.

A scream ripped out of me and I turned away as he

fell, unable to watch him die, no matter the monster he'd become.

He'd thought I wouldn't do it, that I wouldn't hurt him. But he'd killed my cat, and tried to kill me. What did he think was going to happen? That I would just allow him to get away with that kind of behavior?

A sob rippled out of my chest, escaping my mouth, and I clamped a hand over it. I would not cry for Alex. I would not cry for the man who killed Oka. He'd tried to suck my life away, tried to kill me!

But I couldn't separate him from the man I loved.

I forced my feet to move and strode through the thick powdery snow toward the sealed gate of the sylphs' fortress. Using my magic, I magnified my voice, "I've come for the boy!"

Frost? His name was Frost. What was happening, why was I . . .

A flash of black drew my eye to the far right rampart. Raven was here then, trying to keep me from the boy? How little he knew, how little he understood. The boy was mine, was always going to be mine. A child to rule the elemental world, and I would raise him. I would show him how to deal with all these assholes.

Something in me clicked and I finally pushed the compassion I had left in me away. Raven had denied me, and he'd been the one to set me on this path all those years ago. He was not my father. He was just the man who'd knocked up my mother. And she'd died because of it, ultimately.

Hanging on to that anger for all I was worth, I flung a hand toward Raven, using wind to knock him back. He clutched something in his arms. The flash of bare skin and blond hair showed me everything I needed to see. He had the child.

He had Frost. I had to protect Frost, above all else, he was all I had left to protect.

The sylphs rallied along the edge of their fortress, and while I was strong, I wasn't sure I wanted to take them all on alone. There was someone else who could help me with that. Using spirit, I leapt back to where I'd left King, took his hand and ignored the shocked look on his face, then leapt us back to the base of the fortress. "We attack," I said. "Don't stop until the child is in my arms."

King didn't hesitate. He drove his power into the earth and sent a booming tremor that rattled the mountain. The edges of the fortress cracked, ice fell and the snow on the mountain began to slide. The sylphs flew toward us, weapons out, driving the wind ahead of them.

I would show them not to tangle with me ever again.

I smacked my hands, palms together, and a burst of death magic wrapped in flames spewed from my fingertips. Black fire shot out of me and straight toward the sylphs. Most of them dodged it, but two got taken by it. The flames wrapped them up, swallowed them down like a wave, and I amplified their screams that turned into shrieks as their voices shredded along with their bodies. With a snap of my fingers, I dropped their charred and twisted bodies. They looked like nothing more than burnt sticks as they hit the ground.

And they were still alive.

The darkness sucked me down and I reveled in its

power as it hammered against the fortress. I'd kill them all if I had to, to get to the boy. To have him. He was mine.

Mine.

That other voice in me whispered that I was wrong. That this was too much.

I shook my head as pain like a needle jabbed into the side of my skull. Sylphs poured out of the fortress like we'd kicked an ant nest. King laughed and beckoned for them to come at him.

I should protect him. I should protect Mac.

The sylphs rushed him, and he fought them hand to hand and with his elemental magic, turning the snow into water and slamming them with it while I hammered at the fortress. I drove my power into the base of the mountain, feeling its connection to me, feeling the earth tremble when I touched it. The naturally weak spots were easy to find. I could feel them out and I drove my magic into them, cracking them open wide.

I dropped to my knees, shaking hard as the fortress began to tumble. Screams rent the air, so many screams.

I didn't want to do this. I just wanted the boy. "Give him to me, and we will walk away." I amplified the words through the air.

Beside me, King snapped the neck of one of the sylphs, pulling so hard that the bones cracked and gave way, the flesh torn and blood splattered the white snow. I should have been horrified.

Instead I nodded, seeing in him the strength I would need to keep him at my side. "We will keep killing you if you do not give us the boy."

Raven let out a scream from the ramparts and I

watched as several sylphs tackled him and took the child from him.

And then they tossed him over the ramparts, throwing him as if he were garbage, not worth protecting.

Just like Raven had thrown me away.

Like Alex had tossed aside Oka's body.

I cried out and ran for his falling body even as I reached for him with a burst of wind.

I caught him with my power right as he brushed against the cold of the snow. Hurrying, I scooped him up into my arms and cradled him close. "Baby boy, I've got you, I've got you."

He was asleep, his body warm and limp. Had they drugged him? It didn't matter. I had him now. I held him to me, and turned to see King go down under a slew of bodies.

Watched as he was bound and gagged by the sylphs. His eyes met mine and he nodded. As if he understood.

I would come back for him, but I couldn't jump two people at once.

I smiled and blew him a kiss. "Well done, my love. You kept them busy."

I wove spirit through me and the boy and leapt through the Veil away from this place. I stepped out, back to the mountain lake where I'd taken King. Where I'd fucked him.

I shook my head and went to my knees, still holding the boy tight. Still clinging to him as if he would help me remember what I needed to remember.

Frost, his name is Frost.

151

I put him down, and then leapt back through the Veil for King.

The sylphs were not expecting me and I blasted them away from King easily. I touched his shoulder and dragged him through the Veil in a matter of seconds.

"You came back for me," he said as we stepped through to the shore of the lake. "You came back."

I grabbed him by the sides of his face and kissed him, craving the Arctic cold that would remind me of someone. Of something. Of a person who mattered so much to me. Where was he? Why had he left me?

But there was nothing to him except salty water and the cool rush of the ocean. It would have to be enough for now.

I went to my knees in front of the still-sleeping child. "We will show them that we are not to be messed with. I will protect you. I will raise you, you will be mine," I whispered into his soft hair. Taking my cloak from my shoulders, I wrapped it around him and laid him down.

I had one more thing to do. I had to deal with one more problem, one more issue.

There was a cancer that had eaten into me, one that I would dig out and destroy. I had to, for I was sure it was the source of the confusion that kept at me. That confusion inside me had her voice, and her strength when I was uncertain. I had to cut it all away.

I had to face my past once and for all. The past had to die.

15

ALEX

I stood outside the Eyrie, the home of the sylphs, in my four-legged wolf form. A veritable fortress was above me; the square buttresses looked to be carved directly into the mountain itself, both for strength and camouflage. I'd not even realized it was a fortress until we'd been right at the gate that now lowered to the ground in front of us.

Raven had brought me, us, here, jumping the Veil to do so only two hours after Pamela had attacked us. We'd left Oka behind, much to her anger, but she'd understood in the end. We had to get Pamela to where we had the best chance of helping her. Belladonna had taken Oka with her in the hopes that they could be somewhat prepared to meet Pam.

I licked at my chops, tasting the icy snow on my tongue. So much depended on what was left of Pam, how much had been taken over by the darkness. How much could be broken through with the love that we all had for her, and that she had for us.

My right ear flicked as I picked up the sound of feet in the snow behind me as Raven paused and looked back at me. I hadn't wanted to believe that he would be right about Pamela, that she would find my energy first and come for me.

"She's using a darker, deeper magic than I have ever seen. I have no doubt she will find us, but more importantly, she'll find you. You took Oka from her. She believes you killed her familiar. Don't let her think otherwise. Not right away. That rage will make her sloppy." Raven winced as though something pained him, before he went on. "I will have the piglet spelled and under a sleep spell in a very short time, but I have no doubt Pam will be here before I finish. We will have to make a mock fight for the pig, and then we have to let her leave with him."

"And my job?" I figured I already knew but I wanted to be sure, I wanted to know exactly what was needed of me.

"Bait. Keep her busy while I prep the piglet. You'll see me when I'm ready." Raven turned away with a swirl of his black cloak, but not before I saw that same pained look race across his face.

He was losing his daughter, a daughter he'd fought hard to protect, and a daughter I think he loved.

"Not losing her yet, Raven," I said as I lay down in the snow. The big falling flakes covered my back quickly so that only my nose stayed out. I breathed in the air, scenting it, thinking I'd be there for hours yet before Pamela showed.

Wrong again.

Another crunch of feet on the snow caught at my ears a split second before I caught wind of Pamela. My nose twitched; there was something off with her scent, something dark and rank like old blood.

"I know you are here, Alex," she screamed, her voice torn with pain and anger.

I stayed where I was, waiting for the right moment. *Right moment for what? To bop her on the nose?* I could almost hear Oka in my ear. The cat had a point, even when she wasn't with me.

I leapt out of the snow. Pam's blue eyes widened, but otherwise there was little reaction to my appearance. She didn't even brace herself, which wasn't like her. Pam was a fighter, Rylee had trained her. I hit her with both front feet in the center of her chest, knocking her down into the snow. We went down together in a flurry of powdery crystals, as if we'd fallen into a box full of Styrofoam beads. They floated around us and her eyes closed shut tight, squeezing hard. "I can't fight it, Alex," she said.

I lay across her chest and belly, pinning her to the ground, giving her whatever strength and warmth I could. "You have to, Pam, you have to fight whatever this is." What this was, I wasn't even sure. Because there was a chance that Pam was always meant to go dark. Is that what her story was going to be? One of pain, and loss, and the final breaking of her heart so that there was nothing left but rage?

"I love you, Pam." I put my nose under her chin, smelling the other man there. I didn't care, none of this was truly the girl I loved. I would never stop loving her, I would never stop believing in her.

Her eyes squeezed tighter and under me she flexed, her muscles tensing. "I can't stop this from happening. I'm trying, but I can't. I know you wouldn't hurt Oka. Love her for me. You have to end this."

"Stop what from happening?"

Shouldn't have asked that question. Her magic slammed into me and launched me high into the sky, fifty feet at least. I twisted, rolling even while I was still being held high in the air that kept me from falling. Pamela sat up, her eyes flashing with anger and power that crackled along her face.

"You killed my cat. You will pay for that now."

I shifted to two legs, so I could really look at her, make her see me for who I was. "Then you are going to have a fight on your hands, witch."

Her power wrapped around me and I drew it into me, swallowing it down in big gulps, the incubus in me giddy with the strength she offered as if it were on a golden platter. Slowly I was lowered, and I was still sucking the power in. How much could I take? I wasn't sure, but I had to keep her busy. She went to her knees and her eyelids fluttered closed.

I stopped drawing on her and stumbled back through the snow, as if an elastic band had been let go. Power raced through me, power that I had no idea what to do with.

"Pamela," I called to her, not meaning to draw her to me, but I couldn't help it. She stood, her eyes glazed, and she walked toward me, lips parted, the pulse in the hollow of her throat pounding.

I put a hand to the side of her face. She was cold, as if she'd been iced over, and I worried that I'd taken too much from her. But she leaned into my hand, rubbing her face against it. "So warm. A pity I only fucked you once."

And just like that, she flung me out away from her, high into the sky and over the edge of the cliff. I yelled and caught a glimpse of movement on the ramparts of the fortress. The flare of a black cloak and then I was falling, and damn it I really didn't want to die. I twisted in the air, reaching out for something to stop my fall, but she'd flung me too far out. There was nothing but open air and jagged rocks below.

As I fell, the sound of wings snapped my head around. A huge snowy owl swept down through the sky and I couldn't help but reach out for its outstretched talons. There was no way it would be able to catch me, but such is the way of life or death situations: you reached, even knowing the outcome.

Those talons dug into my arms and I was jerked to a stop mid-air, then swung around to a side hill and dropped into a drift of snow. As I fell, I shifted and hit the ground on four legs, and looked up to see the snowy owl land a few feet from me, its eyes a bright green.

Before I could ask who it was that had saved me, the bird shifted to four legs, and sported a spotted snow leopard coat. Peta shook her head at me, rounded ears flicking. "That did not go so well, did it?"

"You could have helped with Pam." I snapped my teeth at her. She didn't growl or even swipe a paw at me.

"And what would you have me do? She cannot hear us right now, Alex. Her world is skewed, she cannot break free."

"She *did* hear me! She told me she was sorry, that she's

fighting!" I yelled. Above us, a boom rocked the mountain, sending a cascade of snow down the hill. I leapt forward racing across the snow to stay out of the way of the avalanche, but that took me further away from the battle that was raging above us.

"Your place isn't here, Alex," Peta said, keeping pace with me easily, seeing as she was ethereal and I was getting sucked down deeper with each leap.

I hit a tree line, and the worst of the avalanche was behind me. "Then why are you here?"

"Because you are. Because I'm trying to help you. You need to be with Rylee now. That is where the final stand will take place . . . but you already knew that, didn't you? Pamela will come full circle, one way or another." She stared at me, her green eyes sorrow-filled.

"No, don't look at me like that, we can save her still!" I yelled the words at her, futile as shouting at the wind for it to quit blowing. "We can save her, Peta. There has to be a way. Tell me, please."

Peta sighed. "Whether she is saved or not is not up to you. That will be a choice she will make on her own. The Mother Goddess . . . believes that Pamela has a greater calling than any of us realized. She is not of any prophecy we thought her to be." She leaned in close, her nose almost touching mine. "She is creating a new path, Alex, and the seers don't know what to make of her. There is no guide post, no understanding of how this will come out."

I stared at the spotted cat. "And you can't do anything? I can't do anything?"

She smiled and her image began to fade. "I already did.

I saved the love of her life in the hopes that he will reach her in time. A faint hope, but hope nonetheless."

And then she was gone, and I was standing in the snow, listening to a battle that I was going to have a bitch of a time getting to.

Gritting my teeth, I spun on my haunches and bounded up the slope of snow, racing between the sparse trees, my eyes locked on the fight ahead. I had to get to her. I had to.

"Don't give up, Pam," I whispered as I leapt up the slope. "Don't you dare give up."

16

By the time I reached the fortress, the fight was over. The sylphs' home still stood, which in and of itself was a fucking miracle as far as I was concerned. Though 'standing' might have been a bit of a generous term. Cracks ran through every column, and fire and smoke curled up into the bright blue sky. Blood splattered the snow, and the sylphs were slowly pulling their wounded back into the fortress.

I shifted to two legs as Raven swept out of the fortress . . . holding Frost by the hand. The little boy looked up at his father. "Where are we going?"

"Yeah, where are you taking him?" I reached for Frost and Raven pulled him into his arms. The boy didn't seem afraid at all. "Raven. What the hell is going on?"

"It has to be all of us, Alex. If she is to have a chance." His throat bobbed as if he could barely speak. "You. Oka. Frost. Me. Everyone that we can gather. We all have to be there to try to break through the hold that the darkness has on her."

"It's dangerous. And you would take him now, after all this?" I growled the words and flung a hand toward the broken fortress. Hating that he would put Frost in front of her after working so hard to keep him away. What a fucking waste!

"I know. But if she hadn't gotten a prize here, she would have destroyed them all, Alex. She wouldn't have believed that he wasn't here. There was no avoiding this confrontation and we managed it the best we could."

I wanted to grab him, but he pinned me with a glare and I thought he would use spirit on me to bend me to his will. "Do it, and I will drain you," I said, keeping my voice as easy as I could for Frost's sake.

"Enough," Raven said. "Pamela is gone. And we have to be ready to meet her. I will take Frost first. We all have to be ready; it won't be long before she goes after the last piece of her family."

Before I could ask him what he meant, he and Frost were gone between one blink and the next. Then Raven was back just as fast. He took me by the arm and the world of the sylphs disappeared.

The world around me wobbled and I sucked in a big breath, the cold of the high mountains gone, replaced with something better. Something like home.

The dusky landscape of the badlands, the ever-blowing wind filling my nose, eyes and ears with dirt—this was where I should have been all along. There was no other place like this, and I would have known it with my eyes closed just by the smell, the feel of it on my skin. The buildings were different, though, not the buildings that had been here before. Not that it mattered, this was the place Pamela would come for her final stand. This was our home.

This was where, if we were going to save her, it would happen.

I saw Liam first, his back to us as he worked over a bench, tools in hand.

"Old man," I said, and he slowly turned. He was blond-haired and blue-eyed and built like a quarterback. Muscular, but made for running.

I grinned when I saw him. As shitty as the day was, I could never not be happy to be home. Even now. These were my people.

And for once, I caught him by surprise, his blue eyes going wide and his mouth dropping open. "Holy shit . . . Alex?"

The door of the main house banged open and the woman who walked out . . . she hadn't changed a bit, not one inch. Long red hair was caught by the wind of the badlands and those piercing, tri-colored eyes locked on me. And then she grinned and was running across the distance between us.

I met her partway, and caught her in a hug, not caring that there were more important things that I had to tell her, but knowing only that we might not get another moment. And then Liam was there and he was hugging me too. I felt the eyes of others on us in the moment, but again, it didn't matter.

"You came home." Rylee grabbed either side of my face and pressed her forehead to mine. "You rotten little shit of a wolf, you finally came home!"

I laughed. "You still have a way with words."

"Once a Tracker, always a Tracker," Raven said softly.

Rylee turned to him, as did I. He had Frost and Oka in his arms. In those few moments he'd jumped to where she was, grabbed her and come back. "Hey, shithead. What are you doing here?" Rylee asked.

I stepped back. "We have a problem."

She beckoned us forward. "Come on then—"

"There isn't time to casually discuss this," Raven said. "Rylee. Pamela has been possessed by the darkest entity in this world. And we don't know if we can bring her back."

Rylee stared at him and then shot a look at me. "Is he fucking serious?"

I nodded. "I can smell the darkness on her. She's blind to it, seems to be working under a perception that is so skewed, she doesn't even know that she's sliding away from us. That she's attacking us."

Oka jumped out of Raven's arms and went to Rylee, standing on her back legs and pressing her front paws against Rylee's knee. Rylee bent and picked her up. "You should be with her, cat."

"I was," Oka said, her voice strained. "And I know just how deep the darkness goes in Pam. It has always been there, but she's fought it in the past using the love she has for her family. For you. For me. For Alex. But something shifted. I don't know if it was the maze she had to go through, or losing Mac, but something changed."

I took a few steps back as Oka told the story of the maze, of Mac's death and coming through to the real world once more. About how Pamela had agreed to help go after Frost, and that she was going to come here next to save Rylee and the others from the elementals. Rylee held up a hand, stopping her there.

"There have been no elementals here. No threat."

Oka sucked in a sharp breath. "Then whatever has a hold on Pam knows her deepest fears and is using them against her. Using her love for her family as a weapon to get her to do what it wants."

Rylee's eyes closed, and she shook her head. "Damn it. She's coming here next?"

Raven, Oka, and I nodded. But it was Raven who spoke. "She is coming here under the pretext that she is saving you, Rylee. That is what the darkness has convinced her of."

Liam folded his arms. "But the darkness will show us as a threat, won't it?"

Slowly, as though it pained him, Raven nodded. "I believe so. Alex here thinks that you will be able to stop her."

Rylee blew out a breath and looked to the sky as if the answer would be there. "I am not Immune to magic any longer. But she doesn't know that. I could fool her and force her to a hand-to-hand fight."

"You could beat her," I said.

Rylee looked at me. "And if I beat her, Alex? What then? Do I kill her? Do I kill a member of my family because she's lost her way?" The pain in her was apparent, no matter that it might be the only way.

My heart sank. "I thought that if you beat her, knocked her out, maybe Raven, you could use spirit . . ."

"There is nothing I can do that will be anything more than temporary," Raven said. "Either Pamela will fight her way out of this when we call to her, or she will not. There is no magic that can force you to give up an addiction to the darkness."

I didn't think my heart could drop any lower, but there it went, hitting well below the ground. "Addiction?"

Raven nodded. "The darkness is seductive in its power, you should know that."

I felt Liam and Rylee's eyes land on me, heavy, questioning. I didn't even hesitate. "I inherited my father's abilities. I am an incubus now. Just for shits and giggles, I didn't lose my shifting abilities either."

Rylee tapped a hand on her leg as the door to the house creaked open. A little girl, no more than three years old with jet-black hair and tri-colored eyes, ran across the yard. "Mama, Zane is not sharing!"

"Mars, back in the house," Liam barked. The little girl slid to a stop and glared at Liam. She put her fists on her hips.

"Wasn't talking to you, *Daddy*."

Rylee turned and faced her daughter. "In the house. Now."

Her tiny shoulders drooped as she spun on a heel and stomped into the house, fists at her sides.

"She's going to be the death of me," Rylee muttered. "How much time before Pamela arrives? Is there any way of knowing?"

Oka bobbed her head. "I can tell you when she's getting closer. She doesn't seem to realize that I'm still alive, but I can feel her. She's a distance away and not moving. The problem is with her jumping the Veil, I can only give you a moment's notice at best."

I held a hand out to Oka and she came to me. "You can let me know, through our bond, and I'll help relay. That work?"

Rylee looked at Liam. "Get everyone else out of here."

He bent and kissed her quickly. "Be careful. I'll be back as fast as I can."

"I've always got a plan," Rylee said.

"Bullshit," I muttered.

Liam barked a laugh and winked at me. "Watch over her for me, wolf pup." Then turned and jogged away.

And just like that, I was home. There was no other place I would rather be. Not even the caravan could bring me hope like this, could bring me a sense of belonging.

I could only hope that the same could be said when Pamela showed up, that this place and the people here would be able to cut through the darkness rolling through her, the darkness that had taken her over.

17

PAMELA

Taking King by the hand, I wove spirit around us both as if I would take us straight to Rylee, straight back to the place where I'd felt the safest. We would leave the mountain lake and I would stop this all madness in my head. I would bring this pain to an end. But I found myself pausing, my hands shaking as though I were . . . afraid?

"Thorn?" Mac's voice flowed out of King's mouth and I turned to him.

"What?"

"Are we going?"

I swallowed hard. I wanted to say yes, we were going. I looked to the small boy asleep, wrapped in my cloak. "I can't leave him here alone." I let King's hand go. "Will you stay with him?"

He slowly nodded. "If you do not think you will need me."

"I might." I might need him, but I didn't know. I just didn't know anything anymore. As I used spirit to leap away from him, I thought I saw him smile at the little boy sound asleep. A smile that sent a chill through my veins.

I changed direction and used spirit to propel me to a place just out of range of King and the little boy, behind a few trees. I leaned out and watched King. He looked around, and not seeing me, went straight to the sleeping child. He crouched over him, hunched like a predator.

"Oh, she will be so sad when she comes back to see that Raven's spell has killed you. But I can't have you reaching adulthood, you're going to be stronger than me. Stronger than her. Stronger than your father." He bent over the boy and pressed his hand over his mouth, pinning him to the ground.

I didn't hesitate, launching myself across the space, and slamming my dark magic into King, lifting him into the air and slowly spinning him to face me.

"Thorn, you came back? Have you finished your fight so quickly?" His voice was smooth and not worried in the least. I'd give him credit for that much.

"You tried to kill him."

"Raven's spell did it. He went too deep with the sleep spell." He gave me a sad smile. "But you and I can have a child. One that is ours."

I glanced down at the little boy, watching in horror as water poured out of his mouth and nose, and then the figure slowly changed from a little boy to a young piglet.

I'd been duped by Raven, and it had saved Frost's life.

Dual rage ripped through me, one for being fooled, and the other that King would betray me. I slammed my power into King, even as tears streaked my face. I was killing Mac. I was choosing to say goodbye to him again.

This was our last chance to be together, but I couldn't trust him.

Only King was not going to go down easy. He pulled on the water of the lake and surrounded me with it, pushing me out into the depths of the cold water. I didn't fight him, just let him push me down while I kept holding him with air.

The water battered at me, trying to force its way into me the way King had killed Rork on the black sand beach. The pressure increased and I closed my eyes. I wove spirit through me and leapt away from the bottom of the lake to stand behind King.

I pulled the air from his lungs brutally fast, hard, enough that everything in him collapsed, but he was not dead. Not yet. I spun him around and stared hard into those dark eyes and spoke with a voice that was not my own. "You gave me what I wanted, undine. A child of power growing in my belly, a child of pure darkness to be molded into all that I see."

His mouth gaped like a fish out of water—an apt description for an undine here, dying because he could not breathe. I smiled up at him, feeling the cold edges of it. "No final words?"

He pulled on the water, but his connection to it was weak as his body failed. The ground rumbled under me and I stilled it with a wave of my hand. "Nice try, but I am the queen here."

His heart slowed and I watched him die, feeling nothing.

Should you not be sad to see him go? To see Mac die again? I wasn't sure if that was Sam or someone else. I shook my head.

"No. There can be no quarter given when loyalty is betrayed. He knew that the child was important to me."

There was no answer to my statement, but I didn't care. I needed to move on. Find the boy, wherever he was hidden now. He was the one I needed. I touched a hand to my belly, and just a flash of a movement flowed through me, a pulse of life. A child.

A child.

I shook my head—I would not be distracted now— scooped up my cloak and yanked it out from under the stiff piglet. It had been dead a long time, spelled to look as though it were a living, sleeping child. "Clever, Raven. But not clever enough."

I wove spirit quickly and took myself away from the lake, away from the mountains. To the place where I would cut out what was left of the emotions in this body. To finally have it to myself.

"Ah, Pamela," I whispered, "you were so foolish to think you could escape me. To think that you stuffed me in an oubliette. What a fool you are."

A whimper rolled through me and I caught it, wrapped it tightly in my anger and put it out like the flame of a single candle. "I look forward to killing the Tracker. And you, do you know what you will see? You will see them attack you. You will see them hate you. And you will destroy them for it. And only then will I let you see the truth." I laughed at the thought of Pamela's heart broken, finally shattered down to nothing, to where I could finally have her for my own.

I wove spirit through me, a tool I'd never had at my disposal before, and leapt the Veil straight to the badlands.

As I stepped out of the Veil, they were there, waiting for me. I knew their names, even though I did not know them. Rylee. Liam. Oka. Raven. Frost. Alex.

"She will never see you as you are now," I said softly. "She is mine. You will not have her."

18

RYLEE

I watched the girl I'd always thought of as my little sister step out of nothing and into the farmyard. She'd grown up, turned into a beautiful woman. Her hair was completely white on one side of her head, the golden strands now silver. What had happened to her? My heart clenched as I thought of all the things she'd been through on her own, unwilling to let anyone in. Unwilling to come home.

"Remember what I said," Raven whispered beside me. "The left side of the heart, it will pin the darkness down long enough to try and bring her back." The thing was, what the fuck did we do if we evicted the darkness? Where would it go? Because I had no doubt that we were far from done with this piece of shit.

Pam's eyes swam with dark blobs that seemed to live there inside, the same as I'd seen in demons. That did not bode well. Fuck, what a way to start the week.

"You think you can keep her?" I grinned at her, my blood pulsing with battle that would be at hand in moments. "You're fucking addled if you believe that. She's stronger than you know."

She grinned back at me, but it was not Pam. This was not our Pam. "Tracker, you think you can face the darkness in me?"

I pulled my swords free. "I'm an Immune, so waste all the energy you want on flinging your shitty excuse for magic around."

"You don't want her dead. So you are at a disadvantage. Because what she sees in her head is that you are attacking her. Hating her. Destroying her. Turning those she loves on her." She motioned with a hand at Oka.

The cat stepped forward, her voice breaking with emotion. "Pamela, you have to stop this. We love you."

A shiver ran through Pamela and she flicked a hand at her familiar, sending her end over end to the far side of the farmyard. "Piss off, cat. I do not need you, nor your affections since you so easily give them away."

Oka cried out where she was, sobbing. "No, Pam, no."

"If you want a fight, then you've got it," I said. I shot forward, my speed more than even she could track. I slammed an elbow into her head and drove her backward. She screeched and went down to one knee, a hand over the eye I'd hit. Hard enough to blind her if I was lucky.

I could only hope Raven was right, that he'd be able to heal her once this was done. I gritted my teeth and pulled my swords from the sheaths on my back. She looked up at me, rage clearly written on her face as she pulled two short daggers from the sheaths on her thighs.

"So be it then."

And the entity that was holding tightly to Pam slid

away, leaving just Pam there to fight me. The girl I loved as a sister, the girl who I'd trained, who'd survived for years on her own. Pain rippled across her face as she rushed forward, her cloak flaring. She took a wide slash at me with her left blade, the edge cutting through the air. I took a step back, went to one knee and drove my blade through her middle. Or I would have if she'd still been there. A crunch behind me was the only warning I had.

I spun on my knees and dropped backward so I was flat on my back as her two blades cut through the air where my neck had been only a second before. From there I rolled to the side. She was using spirit to jump around me.

"Clever," I said, knowing that the blow I had to land was going to be tricky. Left side of the heart.

We danced across the yard, trading blows, landing nicks and cuts, but nothing major. I let her get close to me, and then I feigned a stumble. She came at me harder, pushing to get her blades on me. I dropped one of my katanas, and stumbled again when she kicked me in one thigh. I barely felt the blow.

But she didn't know that.

"You made me do this!" she screamed, tears streaking down her face. "I don't want to kill you, but you've taken them all from me. Even Oka!"

What the fuck was she seeing in her head? Nothing that was real. Nothing that was good.

I caught her own blade as she struck at me, twisted it around and slid the point of it into the left side of her heart. She didn't seem to notice as her other blade rammed up under my arm, going for my heart.

"No!" Liam bellowed, and I heard him but blocked it out.

"Pam." I lifted my free hand and touched her face, wiping the tears away as we both slid to our knees. "Come home to us, Pam." My blood spilled down my side, hot and pulsing fast, but her own fell to the dry ground too, swallowed up in the dusty earth.

Her eyes widened, and her mouth dropped open. "I can't get away. I can't get away."

"Your blades are magic, I told you that," Raven said softly. He caught her as she went all the way to the ground, taking her other blade from her. "You can't shift away with it in your heart."

Her eyes drifted until they were only half closed. "You win then."

I put a hand to my own wound, clamping my fingers over it. "Not yet." The thing was, this wasn't really up to me. This was up to someone else now.

"Alex, you're up."

He went to his knees beside her and took one of her hands in his own. "Pammy, you've got to listen to me, you've got to know how much I love you."

Her eyes fluttered open. Everything happened so fast, even I didn't see it coming. She snapped up her free hand, blade still in it, and drove it into his belly. "If I die, you die."

19

ALEX

The blade drove into my guts, deep, almost out my back. I caught her hand and leaned in to her as Rylee screamed for Raven to do something. It all slid away, all of it.

Because I didn't want to live this life without Pamela. Maybe she was meant to be the one to kill me in the end. With my blood spilling out, I kissed her. Wishing she could see the truth of these last few days, the truth of what had happened.

Oka ran to us and leapt up onto Pam's chest, putting her nose to Pam's. Raven sat behind Pam, held her back to his chest. Liam and Rylee each took one of her hands and little Frost . . . he came and sat beside her. We were bleeding, hurt, wounded, but we were with her, circling her. As much as Rylee and I were hurt, we had to break through to Pam, we had to get her to feel the love we had for her.

Or we would truly lose her.

"Pam," Frost whispered and put a tiny hand on her cheek.

Through it all, the incubus energy in me flared up, taking a little from each of them, not enough to hurt them, and then I reversed it somehow, pushing all that love and energy into Pam. Not to heal her, but to give her the strength she needed to see that we loved her. That we would fight for her to the bitter end if that was what we had to do.

I pulled back enough that I could put my forehead to hers. "You belong with us, Pam, not in the darkness. Don't go there, don't choose to leave."

And just like that she was in my head, seeing my memories as the truth that had truly happened since she'd stepped out of the Veil.

20

PAMELA

lex's memories overwhelmed me, lighting up the inside of my skull like a movie. I saw him try to stop me in the redwoods, saw him holding Oka but not actually killing her, saw him fighting the elementals, saw him pull his shirt off, felt his hands on my body. That hurt in a way that blended grief and regret and shame. I'd always thought I'd be with Alex one day, always thought we'd finally be able to be together, but to have our first time be a sham . . . it left me feeling used. Not by Alex, but by my own magic, my own mind.

All of it, none of the last two days were as I'd thought.

The pain rolling from those who loved me, from those I'd hurt, cascaded through me as I lay there bleeding out, my family holding me tightly. Their love holding me together. Alex's memories showed me everything, of how the darkness had twisted through me, hiding reality from me, showing me what it wanted to, to force my hand.

The truth, the real truth of what was happening flowed through me like a cleansing river. King had not been Mac, that had been a trick of the First Witch to keep me complacent. Oka was not dead. Frost was not dead.

My family didn't hate me.

I saw the moment the First Witch's power had taken me. I could still feel that last moment the First Witch had me as we'd fought, as I'd tried to get her into the oubliette. I'd caught her by the arms and flipped her over my head. *Her magic roared into me, burning my hands, the heat driving into me like dual swords on fire.* There it was, that single moment had changed everything. Her laughter echoed through me. She'd known, that's why she'd let me win so easily; she'd only wanted to touch me, to drive her soul into my body.

For the first time in days, clarity flowed over me. "I don't know what to do." The words slid from my lips, cracked and aching with the pain I'd caused. "I thought I'd stopped her."

"You have to keep fighting her," Raven said.

"I don't know how to fight when I don't know what's real," I whimpered, shaking with the need to feel that dark magic under my skin. Where was Sam?

Sam is no more. I absorbed her.

"She's talking to me." I clung to them, even as Raven healed my wounds. Healed Alex. Healed Rylee. I looked to her first. "Rylee, what do I do?"

She tightened her hold on my hand. "You don't give up. No matter how bad it gets, no matter how fucked up you think things are, you keep fighting. This won't be a single fight; this is a war, Pam."

I wanted to nod, wanted to agree, but I didn't know *how* to fight this. Did I?

"I know what you need to do," Frost said softly, shyly, his fingers against my cheek.

Everyone looked at him and he ducked his head. "My aunty said you need to talk to Griffin. That is what you need to do."

"Griffin?" Raven rocked back on his heels. And then the rest of what the little boy had said seemed to sink in. "Your aunty?"

"Yes, Aunty Larkspur. She said you weren't listening to her." He grinned at our father. "She said you were being stubborn again."

My heart swelled with love for this little boy. "Raven, how long do you think I have, if all of you let go of me?"

"I'll wrap the darkness as tightly as I can," he said, and he worked not only spirit through me, but all five elements. The same way he'd shown me how to create my cloak that allowed me to disappear.

All the elements. I closed my eyes, turning my vision inward as he wove the five elements through me, and around the darkness, turning it into a massively tight ball of energy that writhed inside me. He leaned back and I looked up into his face. Fatigue washed over him.

"Go, you have a little time now."

They all let me go, reluctantly, one at a time. I held onto Rylee when everyone else had stepped back. "I'm sorry."

She tugged me into her arms, wrapping me tightly against her. I was taller than her now, but it didn't matter, I was still the little sister. "You come home to us. That's the deal. We love you, Pam."

"I know," I whispered, but already I could feel the

uncertainty claw at me. If I could be taken so easily by this darkness, what would happen if something else came along? But there was another, worse, darker question that hummed through my skull now that my thoughts were my own. A choking sob curled its way out of me.

Soaking in her love, and all their worry for me, the truth of my situation truly hit me.

I was afraid of the path ahead of me and wanted them to walk it with me. These people were the ones I loved the most—and I needed them—as if I were still that little girl who couldn't decide which path was her own. The sobs slowed as the tears eased and a slow certainty rolled over me. I knew what I had to do, what I was willing to do. Maybe I always had, maybe from the day Rylee had found me shaking in a church in my bright blue socks, I'd been destined to follow this path.

I straightened and pulled away from them all. "I won't let her win, no matter the cost. I won't let her hurt you again. I will make sure of it."

Rylee frowned and reached for me again, but I pulled back another step from them all. Even Alex, though I wanted to tell him goodbye. A proper goodbye. I lifted a hand to him. "I love you, Alex." *But you need to let me go.*

"Pam." Rylee moved to get in front of me. "When this is done, you belong here, with us, with your family."

I had to bite the inside of my cheek to stop the tears from flowing again. "I know you think so, and I think that maybe I did belong here for a little while, so I knew what it was to be loved. You gave me that, more than anyone else. This is always my home. You are always my family but . . ."

Rylee was shaking her head. "No buts, don't you but me."

I managed a smile, feeling the path under my feet shifting, taking me away from her, my one true sister of the heart, from Raven and Frost and Oka. "You taught me, Rylee, how to fight for those I love. How to do anything I had to in order to keep them safe. You're right, I have to keep going."

Oka bounded close and I held up a hand to her. "No. You can't come with me."

Her lower lip trembled. "Pam."

"If I come back, that's different . . . but stay here. Look after my brother. Please." That last word about undid me. I clenched my jaw tight as the tears fell. There were no words for what was between her and me, for the connection, and I knew that if I truly loved her, this was the moment to prove it.

Oka closed her eyes and lay down in the dirt. "You will come back. I will wait for you."

I took another step back, meeting each gaze with one of my own. Saying the goodbyes silently. Because no matter how this outcome with the First Witch happened, I was not coming back.

Thank you, Liam, for showing me what a real man looked like. For helping me believe I had worth and for trusting me in your darkest moment.

Thank you, Frost, for reminding me what it meant to fight for someone you love. Look after Oka, she's going to need you.

Thank you, Alex, for loving me through everything.

For loving me so completely that even now when you should let me go, you don't want to.

Thank you, Raven, for showing me that for some choices there is no good outcome, just the best you can do. For teaching me what you could.

Thank you, Oka, for being everything I could ever want and need in a familiar. You were more than my friend, you were the other half of my soul, and as such I can only set you free.

Thank you, Rylee, for showing me what it was to be brave, to do what you had to when you were terrified.

Thank you, all of you, for loving me, even in my darkest moments.

I wrapped my cloak around my body and wove spirit through me, leaping to the last place I knew Griffin to be.

The redwoods of the terralings.

21

RYLEE

Pamela disappeared with a swirl of her cloak, gone in a flash from our lives. "She's not coming back." Liam wrapped an arm across my shoulders and tugged me to his side. I couldn't take my eyes from the spot she'd been standing only moments before.

"She'll be back," I said with more certainty than I truly felt. Because there had been a moment when we'd bled together that I saw the darkness in her and it was awesome in the most terrifying of ways. Like looking into a pit of demons that knew you were looking as they leered back.

Alex was on his knees. I put a hand on his shoulder. He flinched and I tightened my hold on him. "No, you don't get to pull away now. I don't give a flying fuck what you are. You are Alex. End of the fucking story."

He leaned his face against my thigh like he had so many times as a mixed-up werewolf at my side. I moved my hand to the side of his face and just held him as he cried. There was nothing I could do, nothing at all, and it galled the shit out of me.

"Raven—" I said.

"No. We have done what we can." He scooped up Frost and made his way to my other side.

I looked at him, really looked at him, and didn't like what I saw. "What have you done?"

Alex went still next to me, listening. Raven sighed. "You couldn't understand, not even if I explained it to you."

I looked at him, looked at Frost in his arms. "You know what? I have a little girl your age. Would you like to go play with her?"

Frost nodded but Raven didn't put him down. "I've lost one child today; you'd take the other?"

I slowly made my way around to face him. "You did this. I don't know how, but you did this. Didn't you?"

He shook his head. "I don't know what you're talking about."

"I know a fucking liar when I see one!" I snapped. Frost looked at me, then at his father.

"Put me down."

His father let him slide out of his arms, a strange, glazed look in his eyes. Oh, shit.

The child jogged away, Oka torn between trailing him and hearing what Raven had to say.

Liam gave me a look. "I'm on it."

He followed the boy and I faced Raven. "What did you do? Why couldn't Lark reach you?"

The thing was, Raven could have jumped the Veil like Pamela and escaped my questions, but he didn't seem to have it in him. Maybe it had taken more out of him than he'd thought it would, binding the darkness in Pam. "I had to. You have to understand there was no other way. Pamela is the only one strong enough. The only one."

Chills swept up and down my spine. "Strong enough to . . . what? To beat her?"

Had he set this up? What the fuck had he done?

I pulled a sword slowly and rested it against his neck. Blue eyes stared up at me, the exact same shade of blue as Pamela's. Beside me Oka shifted into her other form, a massive tiger. A low rumble escaped her.

"What did you do, Raven?"

"The First Witch would have found her way into this world. There was no stopping her. There is only one way to truly contain her." He didn't look away from me. "Some choices, no one will understand why you make them, Rylee. Some choices are just messed up from the beginning to the end. How do you save everyone from the darkness? How? You tell me if there was a better way."

My hand trembled. "Goddess above and below . . . you did this. Didn't you? You gave Pamela to the First Witch?"

Raven closed his eyes.

"There was no other way. Even Lark knew that."

Oka roared and tackled Raven, sending him end over end until he was flat on his back and she was on top of him, her teeth bared. "You . . . sacrificed her?"

Raven stared up at her, not fighting. "If the First Witch was set free on this world, there would have been no stopping her for a thousand years, maybe more. Not even the demons would have escaped. Do you understand? One life, for a thousand years."

I actually stumbled where I stood, because I couldn't believe he would do this. At my side, Alex sat there on his ass, staring out over the badlands. "I agree with him."

I stared down at him. "What the fuck did you just say?"

He looked up at me, golden orbs still wet with tears. "I agree with him. If anyone can do this, if anyone can stop the First Witch, it's Pam. But it's all on her now. We can't help her."

"Slippery bastard!" Oka snarled and I whipped around. Raven was gone.

"He's got the kid!" Liam yelled as he ran out of the house.

I closed my eyes. "Okay, Pam, this is on you. Time to pay the piper and kick some ass."

22

PAMELA

As I stepped into the redwood forest one more time, I wondered if I would ever come back here.

"Griffin, Lark sent me to you," I called out as I took a step, and then another. There was no reason to take any one path, so I just kept going east. The way the caravan had been headed.

My heart and throat clenched thinking of all the people waiting on me. Thinking I would get them to safety.

"I don't know. I just don't know." I rubbed my hands over my face, worry eating at me. The ball of darkness in me stretched and pulled at its bonds, anger lashing out. I didn't go far before I found a tree large enough that would be as good a place as any to wait. My body and heart were exhausted. I hadn't slept once in the last two days, and I was feeling it.

I slid down the side of the tree, eyes closed and head leaned back as I tried to slow my racing heart. The feeling that I was letting time slip by—doing nothing about stopping the darkness in me—sent a rush of anxiety through my veins.

I clung to the love of my family, still feeling their touch, their faces and hope in their eyes. They believed in me.

"Is there nothing I can do at all?" I said softly. The bushes farther out from me bent and moved as a massive black wolf with a scar over his face stepped through them. He made Alex look like a pup in comparison.

In another time, Griffin had claimed to be the consort of the Mother Goddess. I'm not sure exactly what he was, but he had a lot of wisdom and had been around a very long time.

"Hello, Griffin," I said. "You heard me call then."

He let out a low growl and snapped his teeth at me. I shrugged and pointed a finger at him. "Don't act like you're shocked that I'm here. Lark sent me."

The wolf tipped his head to one side, showing off the gray hairs around his muzzle and along the center of his chest. A slow wolfy grin slid over his face, showing off a good set of bright white teeth. He sat and gave a full-body shiver.

There was a moment where I sat across from a wolf, and then in the next I sat across from a grizzled, salt-and-pepper-haired old man with a lanky build. He was at least wearing clothes, which I was grateful for, even if they did look more than a little beat up.

"Pamela, little witch, hey?" He grinned and shook his head. "What are you doing here?"

"You got old," I said.

He barked a laugh. "Yup, I did. And you didn't change that mouth of yours, did you?"

I shook my head. "I had a moment where I thought I was coming around, but I think that maybe the world needs me the way I am, not the way some people would like me better."

That is the truth, girl. What felt like Sam laughed quietly in the back of my head. Maybe she was back now that the darkness was bound? *You can be strong and still cry. Sometimes the strongest you can be is when you are sobbing your heart out. That is the last piece of advice I can give you. The First Witch will break free and then I will be gone for good.*

If I could have, I would have hugged her. I never thought I would be grateful to have that magic speak to me again, but I was. I gave myself a little shake, realizing that Griffin had asked me again what I was doing there. I put a hand to the earth, feeling the warmth and the power there.

"It's complicated," I said. "But Lark sent me, so why don't you tell me why I'm here."

"Because you can't find your way past the darkness? Because you're afraid of the path in front of you?" He grabbed a piece of grass and twiddled it between his fingers. "That's the problem, we don't always be liking the way our options show up, hey? Maybe we just make the best of it."

He put one end of the grass in his mouth and chewed on it, but the glitter in his eyes told me he wasn't done yet.

"What do you know, Griffin? Are you helping me, or setting me up for a trick?" I wiggled my fingers, and using air, picked up a dozen rocks, spinning them lightly in the air between us.

"Ah, I don't never mean to be tricksy," Griffin said. "But sometimes you can't say what you can't say, hey? We all have secrets. We all have things we are bound to keep to ourselves whether we want to or not. Like you and that darkness you carry around with you now. Not that it's a secret now, is it, hey? Everyone knows you carry the First Witch in you. Raven knew for a long time, didn't he?"

My jaw dropped open. "No, Raven didn't know. How could he?"

His eyes widened. "You think he *doesn't* know? You, the daughter of the Raven, don't realize when he's been leading her along by the nose, hey?"

I just stared at him, a pulse of anger cutting across the bonds he'd used to wrap the darkness up. "You're telling me—"

"That Raven has known all along. He's been playing you and everyone else. Again." Griffin raised both brows. "Tell me you're not surprised."

I was and I wasn't. "Hurts," I said after a moment. "I thought we were beyond the games."

So what was I doing here then?

He sighed. "I don't think he has it in him not to play games. Just like it's not in you to give up. Even when you are carrying a powerful parasite."

Oh, he did not just call me a parasite, did he? This from a wolf who is probably full of shit worms.

Sam's indignation bled through into me, but I pushed it down, because it wasn't really Sam. There was a subtle

191

difference to the voice this time, a thickness that made me want to scrub my arms.

"You can't wash it off," Griffin said. "You gots to learn to live with it. And quick, hey?"

A shiver ran through me and a few of the bonds that Raven had wrapped around the darkness snapped wide. I had to hurry and my words spilled out faster than I could filter them. "Frost . . . no, Lark, said that you could help me. That you were my best chance at dealing with this."

Griffin's eyes looked me up and down, not in a sexual way, but like he was trying to figure me out. "I don't have all the answers, little witch. You might think so 'cause I've been around a long time, but even the Mother Goddess don't know all the answers, hey?"

"Then why the fuck am I here?" The words were shouted, half strangled, wrapped in fear and self-loathing. "The First Witch is in me and I . . . I don't know what to do."

"Funny when you think about that. You didn't ask me how to get rid of her. Telling, very telling." He smiled sadly, like his laugh had been sad. "I know what you're really asking, and the Mother Goddess knows too. You have a path that I do not envy you, Pam." His smile slid from his face. "You've accepted your blood magic, and you've accepted the power of the elementals that flows through you."

"Yes, but—"

He lifted a filthy hand to stop me. "There is more to you than that, hey? More than just magic and power. There is this willingness to do what others believe is impossible. Raven was like that when he was younger, and

I helped him where I could—because everyone thought him the villain. Just like they think he's the villain now. You think he's the villain, don't you?"

"He set me on this path—"

"And what do you think would have happened if you didn't step into the path of the First Witch? Who would she have taken?" Griffin tipped his head to one side. "Who would she be controlling right now?"

I swallowed hard. "The young witch I faced. The one who looks like me."

"Right-o. And that little witch has no love to balance the darkness. She's hidden in your caravan now, and if you let her stay there she will become their caravan witch. There is nothing in her that can keep the First Witch in check. Even here, I see you struggling and succeeding to keep the darkness at bay. You've spent your whole life doing it, so you are uniquely designed for this . . . job."

"Goddess above," I whispered, his words sinking into me like hooks I couldn't escape. "What are you saying? That . . . I need to keep it? I need to keep the darkness? How can I live like that? How can I go on with my life if I'm . . . a monster?" I couldn't keep the panic from my voice, from the way it pitched upward as what he was saying truly sunk into me.

His eyes stared into mine, holding me there even as the desire to get up and run away cut through me, to put this place behind me and go back to the caravan. To bury my head in the sand and pretend nothing was wrong. But I couldn't, not with the First Witch inside me, waiting. Not with the darkness wanting to kill those I loved.

Griffin held a hand out to me, palm up, and I slowly

put my hand over it. His fingers engulfed mine. "Tell me your journey, Pamela. Has it been all roses and sunshine?"

"No, of course not. It's been . . ." I rubbed a hand over my face. "It's never been easy. There has always been a draw to the dark for me, to doing things . . . hard." I thought back to when Rylee had first found me, how willing I'd been to fight at her side even though I was barely fourteen. I'd been willing to kill. I'd done things that should have marred me more but they hadn't, because I'd always been willing to walk a path shaded from the light.

Griffin's hand tightened over mine and he covered it with his other one, holding me gently. "And since you've been with the caravan? What about that?"

Slowly I looked up at him. "What are you saying?" What did the caravan have to do with this darkness?

He sighed, as if I should clearly see the connection. Maybe I was just too overwhelmed, maybe I didn't want to see. "Tell me. Please."

"From the moment you joined the caravan, your feet have been on this path. The First Witch was testing you all along, pushing you to use your darker magic, seeing what you were made of. She never wanted you dead, Pamela. I'm sure of it, as I'm sure that the sun will rise tomorrow, hey?"

Every battle over the last few months came back to me. What I'd had to do to keep the caravan alive. Kill. Torture. Lie. Manipulate. "I . . . was keeping them safe." I whispered the words because they were a slim defense against what was clearly in front of me. Of what I'd become without even realizing it.

Griffin's smile was sad, but he still smiled. "There always has to be balance, Pamela. The Mother Goddess knows this."

"What are you saying?" I asked the same question, feeling like he was on the verge of spitting it out. I needed him to say it, I needed the words to actually be in the air between us.

"I'm saying that perhaps Frost and this world doesn't need another hero, Pamela." His grip tightened on me. "Perhaps we need a villain like no other."

23

PAMELA

I stared at Griffin, my hand trapped in his strong hold, the wind blowing softly around us and through the redwoods. His words echoed through my head, over and over.

A villain like no other.

I could barely breathe, the weight of what he was asking of me settling on my shoulders.

"I don't . . . I'm not strong enough for what you're asking. You think I can somehow *control* the First Witch? All that power? The last day and a half she's run fucking rampant through my life! She's had me fucking men I didn't know, fucking men I did, sent me on a mission to kill my family and I let it all happen! How can I possibly be strong enough?" I was yelling and pulling on my hand, but he didn't let me go. He shushed me.

"Raven has always known there was a possibility of the darkness being unleashed, especially if the Veil was torn and all the old bonds were stripped bare." He shook his head slowly. "There are no prophecies surrounding you that we know of, at least concerning this." He paused and I thought he muttered 'guardian' under his breath, but he shook his head.

"No, there was, I'm supposed to be a guardian." I was desperate to find a way out of where this conversation was going. Of the direction my life was going.

He tipped his head back, looking up to the tops of the trees. His throat bobbed as he spoke. "Guardian can mean many, many things. A crown of darkness was something bandied about but it wasn't a full prophecy, just people talking, hey? But we always knew that the First Witch could get free, that it could happen. She's like the Mother Goddess, not immortal, not mortal, something in between. Something more elemental in nature, part of the balance."

Griffin gave a sharp pull, dragging me on my knees closer to him so that we were almost nose to nose. A low growl rumbled out of him, and straight into me, resonating in my chest.

"What are you—"

"There is power in the darkness, Pamela," Griffin whispered. "And we are at another tipping point. If the elementals have their way, we will all be enslaved or killed. They will rule violently with no care for those they should be watching over. In this moment, right now, they are bound together to deal with the threat. Remove that threat? And you will have them warring with one another. There are not enough other supernaturals to face them. Even Rylee cannot stop them."

I couldn't move, all I could do was stare at him as my mouth went dry and my heart thumped uncomfortably in my chest. "You want . . . *me* . . . to be the villain? You want me to be the one that everyone hates, to keep the world safe?"

His eyes pooled with tears and that was as terrifying as his words. "Yes. I want you to embrace all the darkness, to be strong enough to keep the elementals in their place. To keep them from reaching for more." He paused and did a long blink. "They have to be afraid of you, Pamela. They cannot be the top of the food chain."

Part of me understood what he was saying, the other part was fighting it tooth and nail.

"But Raven, isn't he strong enough to be the bad guy? He was before."

Griffin nodded. "Yes, when he had the jewels, they helped him. But those jewels are scattered, some broken; and even if he had them, I'm not sure it would be enough, hey? He's not the man he once was." I didn't think he could pull me closer without kissing me, but I was wrong. He tugged me forward so that his mouth was against my ear. "The elementals are planning a war, Pamela. A war just like the humans planned wars. There is no check in place. No way to make them stop. Unless you take up all that you could be. The darkness is enough to stop them. The darkness is enough to keep them preoccupied. That is your job. Keep them busy for as long as you can."

He let me go and I fell backward, hardly realizing that I'd been leaning away from him while he'd held me. I scrambled backward and up onto my feet. "You're mad."

"No. I'm broken, just like you are broken. You have a choice, little witch." He shifted back into his wolf form. "What are you truly willing to do, what cost are you willing to pay to assure the safety of those you love? Are you willing to die for them?"

"Yes." Without hesitation that word fell from my mouth.

"To damn your soul? To let them hate you and all you are?" he asked.

I swallowed hard and the tears started anew, because I knew the answer. "Goddess forgive me, yes. For them I would give it all, whatever was asked of me."

He bobbed his head. "The First Witch is no fool. Negotiate, Pamela. Negotiate for control."

Just like that, our conversation was over. With a flick of his bushy tail, he trotted away into the trees, disappearing like a ghost.

My knees buckled and I went to the ground, hunched over myself.

What I wouldn't give to have Oka in that moment, to scoop her into my arms and feel the strength of her soul, the strength of her rumbling purr. All I could do was cry, sobs wracking my frame as Griffin's words crashed through me. He wanted me to go dark to save people. To save Frost and the caravan, to stop the elementals, to keep Rylee and my loved ones from harm.

To negotiate with the witch.

A footstep brought my head up. Standing in front of me was someone I did not expect to see, not by a long shot. Two someones.

"Crimson, what are you doing here?" I looked past her. "Dick."

Richard saw me and ran forward, scooping me up off the ground. "Oh, Pamela, you're back!"

Back. I patted his arm and he put me down. "Why are you two here?"

"The whole caravan is here. Just resting, because there isn't enough safety for us all," Crimson said. "The kids are having fun though, checking out the forest. Lots of life here, lots of potential."

A few more cracks rippled through me, layers of the bonds Raven had laid around the darkness giving way. Laughter, madness, flowed with it.

Soon enough.

"Come on, everyone wants to see you!" Richard tugged on my hand and I . . . saw inside his head, like I'd seen in Alex's.

Stunned, I just stared at him. "You are a servant of the First Witch."

He paled and his throat bobbed. "How—?"

"You set me up for her. You found me because she sent you into my path. To test me." Each layer peeled away and I saw it all. He was human, but influenced by the darkness that had been seeking me. "You really are a dick."

He looked at the ground. "I didn't have a choice, Pamela."

I nodded, seeing the cost to him in trying to escape the First Witch. That was what had killed his wife, not the bungling of Sage's herbs gone awry.

And for that I just let him lead me away. I was quiet as they filled me in on things. Things that I'd seen in Alex's memories. I followed them, though, wondering how long I had where I was still me.

How in the bloody hell was I going to negotiate with the First Witch?

I didn't even know. What could I possibly have to negotiate with?

A thought came to me and I shoved it away, hard and fast. No. I would not offer that. Not him.

"Here, everyone, Pam's back!" Richard crowed out to the caravan as we came around a massive big redwood, as if he'd not just admitted to being the First Witch's pawn.

The caravan swarmed us, they were there, all of them. The humans and shifters, the children, all the people I'd worked so hard to keep alive.

They came at me fast, hugging me, some of them even crying, and then I was crying too because this was a goodbye I didn't want. I didn't want this. I didn't want to be the bad guy. The villain. I didn't want to be the darkness to offset the light.

And maybe that was the best reason to do it, because I didn't want it. I would never willingly go bad. I wiped my tears away. "I've missed you all, more than I could have thought." A shuddering breath cut through my words and I saw more than a few people look down and wipe their eyes. Even Chris had tears on her cheeks. I smiled at her and she nodded at me, the past forgotten in that one gesture.

I didn't want to leave them when they were still hunting for the—

"The Haven doesn't exist," Richard whispered in my ear. "I've always known it, Pamela, but I needed them to believe in something bigger than themselves to keep them going. But this place . . . it feels like it could be a haven. Do you think it's safe enough? Can you make it safe enough?"

I licked my lips, a thought coming back to me, something Raven had done. "Do you all love it here?"

He grinned wide. "It's got everything we need. Shelters, food, water, and pretty good neighbors."

Of course, the terralings weren't far . . . but maybe that would be a good thing. A safety net, a new beginning.

I started forward. "Then this will become the Haven, the place of safety. Where is your new witch?"

The weight of everyone's eyes should have slowed me, but the truth was, if there was nothing good to come of embracing the darkness, then there was no point and I might as well give up now. I had to find a balance for myself, and not just the world.

Jess, my little look-alike, came forward. "I am their caravan witch now."

I nodded, knowing that this was the only lesson she'd get from me. But it was a lesson that would serve her well. "Watch what I do. Learn."

I opened myself up to spirit, let it flood through me first. Then one by one, I fed the other elements into it, weaving it tightly, and with an ease that I'd missed. My magic was its own homecoming I'd barely been able to appreciate since the bands on my wrists were taken off. The same way I'd woven the magic into my cloak, I wove this new thread into the earth, into the trees and the plants, into the roots and the stream. I pushed it wide, opening myself more and more.

This was for those I loved, for those I'd fight and die for. What was my magic if I couldn't keep them safe?

Nothing, it was nothing.

The darkness in me rose higher, and I let it come, weaving it into the spell, strengthening the bonds and sending them out farther, farther than the scope of the trees, and onto the edge of the mountain range. Landmarks, I needed landmarks and I found them in nature.

Could I go farther? The question rolled around in me and I wondered, truly wondered how strong I was, but even this distance would be enough for a long time. Long enough.

I let it go and fell to the side. Richard caught me. "Pam, what did you do?"

"From the forest to the mountains' foot, to the shattered rocks to the crashing white waterfall and back here, this is your Haven. Hidden from the world. But you must welcome those who mean no harm."

A cheer rose up with the group and I let go of Richard, stepping back. The three original remaining children saw me, but it was Ruby who lifted a little hand and waved. She knew I was leaving. I waved to her and blew her a kiss. She would be a force one day, I could see it in the light around her, like a halo. Crimson stood next to her, a protector, a familiar.

Would I face Ruby one day? Would she hate me? I pushed those thoughts away. Today was not the day, today I had to keep moving knowing that I was doing some good.

A few lives saved. That had to be worth the cost.

I hurried to leave the haven, and they let me go. They

didn't try to stop me, so busy with their celebrations that they didn't notice I was no longer there. It was better that way. I stepped over the boundary line and wrapped spirit through me, leaping away to the crystal clear mountain lake.

I had negotiations to make with a witch.

24

"Sam."

Are you speaking to me?

The crisp air of the mountain valley swept through my hair as I stared out across the lake. "Yes, I'm speaking to you."

"My name is Xa."

I turned slowly to see the First Witch on my left side.

"Xa is a shit name. I prefer Sam."

Her eyebrows slowly raised and a smile slid over her lips. "Fine, call me Sam then."

I nodded. "You need me."

"I need a body," she acknowledged. "I could take the other witch."

"She's weak."

"True."

"And young."

"A point in her favor," Sam said. "But yes, you interest me more."

"You mean I have power you don't." My words were

dry. "Don't beat around the bush. What do you want to allow me to stay semi-autonomous?"

I quelled the instant panic that clawed at me. I wanted more than that. I wanted a life . . . but I could feel my path under my feet, and Griffin's words. I knew what I had to do.

"The boy. I want to raise the boy." She crossed her arms.

"Why?"

She smirked. "Because I do."

I rolled my eyes. "Fucking hell, it's like talking to a teenager! Tell me why you want Frost."

There was no push and pull of power, so I suppose I could be grateful for that.

"What is this place? I like it," Sam said, looking out over the water.

I wrinkled my nose. "This is our home. No one will bother us here."

"Excellent," she whispered. I had to keep my thoughts to myself, so she wouldn't see my long-range plan.

Maybe my father was right to have chosen me.

"Why Frost?"

"Because he can bring the elemental world under one ruler. A ruler I will mold."

I pinched the bridge of my nose. "But why?"

"Because I am evil incarnate. You know that. Why else would I do something other than to cause grief?" Her words were smooth and well delivered, but there was some other reason, I was sure of it. I tried to dig through the thoughts that spun in my head, grasping at the words that were hers, that I thought were hers. But it was not her voice that bled through my mind.

The Mother Goddess's warmth lit me up from the soles of my feet to the crown of my head.

Balance. This is about balance. This world cannot have light and no dark. The threads would untie and the world would crack into nothing. That cannot be allowed, you must hold the balance. You must be the darkness, Pamela. No one else can know, no one else can understand. The fight between good and evil, between light and dark is eternal, and is how we define our souls, it is the energy that keeps the world alive. There can be no light without the dark, Pamela. I made a place for you, a place of safety, a place of balance.

I could see the crystal lake within the mountain valley. Created for me, because the Mother Goddess had always known I would need my own sanctuary. Her words sank into me in a way that none of Griffin's had.

There could be no light without the dark.

A full-bodied shiver rolled through me and I found myself steeling my spine for what I was doing. Knowing that the Mother Goddess was still there, she still would be my rock when I needed her. Warmth spread up through my legs again, confirmation of her connection to me. But Sam seemed oblivious to her.

I schooled my face. "If I bring Frost here, and I raise him, you will allow me to—"

"You will be free to be who you wish to be. The darkness will shade your mind. Maybe not right away, but in not too many years you will forget who you are. You will become the thorn I know you to be."

"Why didn't you just take me?" I blurted the question quickly, like tearing the scab off a wound.

"I tried." She shrugged. "You have too much love in your heart for me to just take you. They proved that time and again, no matter how hard I tried to break you. So I will take what I can get, knowing that in time I will wear you down."

I put a hand over my mouth.

Their love had saved me, even now. "How long before the darkness fully takes me?"

Sam pursed her lips as she held a hand out to me, blood welling in her palm. "Years. It will depend on how strong you are. How much you decide to fight me. How tired you get."

I looked down at my palm and pulled one of my curved blades with the other. I pressed the knife against my palm, cutting open a shallow wound.

"I will bring you Frost. You will allow me control of this body and its decisions with only the influence of the darkness."

"Deal." She grabbed my hand so quickly that I knew I'd forgotten something, I had to have forgotten something. But as her image turned into smoke, and that smoke wove its way into the wound in my palm, I knew it didn't matter.

The deal was struck, and my path was set.

It was time to get Frost.

To not be afraid of what was to come. I wove spirit through me, thinking about just what I was going to do.

How I was going to get Frost away from the others.

And I knew that I would have only one person who would support me, who would see me through this.

Oka.

I leapt directly to her, knowing I was taking a chance. I popped out of the Veil at the back of a building that I was sure was the barn on Rylee's farm. Oka lay with her eyes closed, tears trickling down her soft fur-covered cheeks.

I crouched beside her. "I was wrong, Oka."

Her eyes flew open and just as quickly she was in my arms, licking my face. "Pam, Pam, you came back!"

"Shhhh," I whispered, holding her tightly to me. The darkness in me grumbled about stupid pets.

"Shut it, Sam," I snarled.

Oka pulled her head back and put a paw on each of my cheeks. "What's going on? I thought Sam—"

I filled her in quickly on my visit with Griffin, the caravan, and now what I planned to do. And why. "I understand if you can't, if you don't want to come with me. This will be hard and everyone will hate us."

Those chartreuse eyes never looked away from me. "Peta was right, you are harder to deal with than Lark. At least all she wanted was to destroy the world. You want to bloody well rule it."

A laugh curled out of me before I could catch it. "I don't. And I'll be fighting every day to keep the darkness in check." I lifted her onto my shoulder. "Raven is still here?"

"No. Shit for brains ran away the first opportunity that came. And he took Frost with him."

"Hush," I touched her on the side and her tail curled

around my wrist, "I understand him, even though I wish I didn't."

"We do this together," Oka said. "And if you ever try to leave me again, I'm going to claw your face when you're asleep."

"Duly noted," I said, and then I stepped out around the side of the barn. There would be no understanding from Rylee, Raven, Alex and Liam for what I would do next. Not from any of them. But it didn't mean I didn't love them. It didn't mean I wasn't fighting for them, for their safety.

It only meant that I was going to do what it took, no matter the cost.

No matter if it meant being the most dangerous villain this world had ever seen.

25

I took Oka through the Veil to the swamp where Raven had taken us at the beginning of this journey. Three days, barely three days had passed and yet a hundred years could have gone by with not as much happening in a single life.

I lifted the water underneath me and used it to float us across the swamp to the edge of Raven's home.

"Why didn't you do that before?" Oka muttered.

"Didn't think about it then." I smiled, feeling weirdly comfortable with what was about to happen. Maybe that was the darkness. Or maybe it was the bloodline I shared with Raven, one that made me willing to make that hard choice.

To take whatever you had to for the greater good.

Sam sniffed. *You're delusional already.*

I stepped off the water and into the haven he'd created. Frost saw me first.

"Pam!"

He was running for me when Raven scooped him up.

"I've come for Frost," I said softly.

"No."

Anger crackled through me and I pushed it down, quelling it quickly. "You chose to put me on this path and I made a deal with the devil to keep my mind. But there is a price to pay, Raven. You know that, don't you? There is always a price to pay to serve the world what it needs. Not what it wants."

His face crumpled. "I can't lose you both."

I smiled. "Then you will come with us."

Inside me, Sam raged. *No, that was not the deal!*

Oka laughed. "Oh, I can hear her screaming!"

Raven looked between us. "What?"

Oka leapt off my shoulder and shifted into her tiger form before she landed. "The darkness has a name, and it's Sam. Sam is pissed off because she thought Pamela would steal Frost away."

I gave Oka a nod. "I have a plan, Raven. But you have to trust me."

He stared at me. "You're serious?"

I nodded. "Come with me. Help me stay steady. Raise Frost safely." My lips trembled. "Don't make me walk this path alone."

Oka pressed against my leg and I dropped a hand to her. She was here, and while that meant the world to me, I wanted more. I wanted a family.

Sam writhed inside me but I pressed the darkness back. Not easily, but Griffin was right: all those years of fighting myself made it second nature to bat it down. And a blood promise was enough to bind the magic.

Raven scooped up Frost and walked past me into the swamp.

"You going to make sure he doesn't make a run for it?" Oka asked quietly.

"He won't." I turned to follow him.

"How do you know?"

I stepped out of the swamp. Raven waited for me. I smiled. "Because we are cut from the same cloth, and I would wait."

I told him of the mountain pass, where the crystal lake was, and then I jumped Oka and myself there, trusting him.

A moment later, Raven stepped out of the Veil, holding a still-smiling Frost. Raven put him down, and he and Oka ran for the water's edge.

"How do you not hate me?" Raven asked as we stood side by side and stared over the lake.

I shrugged. "I hate that you don't trust me, Raven. From here on out, no matter how much you think I won't like it, you tell me what your plans are. Because I would have chosen this path if you'd told me back at the caravan. And I wouldn't have had to do . . . so much harm." To myself, as much as to others. I could still feel King's touch on my skin and it made me shudder.

"I wasn't sure," Raven said. "I wasn't sure then that this would be the outcome. I didn't want to lose you."

I nodded. "I think I would like to take the name my mother gave me. I'm not really Pamela anymore, the girl that Rylee saved, the girl that is so afraid that she lashes out, the girl that can't look the darkness in the eye."

He held a hand out to me and then pulled me into a side hug. "Thorn."

Thorn.

"Now," I said, letting him go, "let's make this place a haven like no other."

26

ALEX

One Year Later

THE FARM WAS BUSTLING WITH ACTIVITY AND I LET THE noise and smells roll over me. I lifted my nose and breathed it in from where I stood watch on the far edge of the homestead.

"You ever going to shift back to two legs?" Liam walked up to me from the eastern edge.

I shook my head. "Maybe. I don't know."

Liam didn't push. Rylee would have and we'd had more than a couple of fights over the fact that I didn't want to be on two legs right now. Being a man got me into more trouble than I wanted to remember.

And I so badly wanted to remember her.

I shook my head and jogged off, away from the farm. I should have been happy, should have been settled.

But I couldn't forget Pam, even now, knowing what she'd done. First, she'd created a massive haven that even now was helping the humans find a footing in our world, somewhere that magic of any kind was suppressed. Then the other rumors.

Darker rumors had turned into truth within a few months, evidence that the terralings had brought us. Because Pamela had shown up and told them. She'd taken Frost and killed Raven to do it.

I couldn't be terribly upset about Raven dying . . . but to take the little boy? It made my guts twist to think just how and what she might have done to him. What she planned for his future.

Following a path I knew like the back of my hand, I found my way to a tiny hollow under a stack of rocks that I curled up near. I'd been keeping watch all night and needed a few hours' sleep. I'd learned quickly that being too near the house meant that the ogre brats would find me in no time.

A grin slid off my wolfy lips as I fell asleep, tail tucked over my face.

And woke in a dream world.

With Pamela standing across from me. Her hair was completely white now, and her body had curves I didn't remember. Fuller. Softer. Not so hard from surviving, but so beautiful. A long flowing dress made of the darkest blue clung to her. Lace across her arms and around her feet. Bare feet. The details were all I could notice.

I closed my eyes. "I can't do this again. Every time I close my eyes you haunt me."

"I know. But I want . . . I miss you, Alex." Her hand

brushed my cheek. "I know what it would mean for you to walk away from Rylee and the others now, but . . ."

My eyes flew open and I realized this was the place we'd been before, the place of dreams. "You . . . you're really here?"

She nodded and I pulled her to me, kissing her hard and just hanging onto her. She kissed me back and I didn't care that she'd done so much . . . I knew her soul inside and out.

She pulled back a little, her hands coming up to my face. "Come with me, Alex. Please."

I drew in a sharp breath. "I . . . I don't know."

She nodded, tears welling up in her eyes. "I understand. I do. But I had to ask. I would never forgive myself if I didn't ask."

I didn't let her go. "I have to say goodbye to them."

Her mouth dropped open. "What?"

"I have to say goodbye to Rylee. I can't just leave. I can't hurt her like that."

She threw herself at me, her arms going around my neck as she cried. "I thought you . . ."

I hung onto her, breathing her in, knowing that I was damning myself by going to her. Rylee might understand, but others wouldn't.

The world wouldn't.

I let Pam go, and she shook her head. "I can't bring you here. You have to come to me, Alex. I'll explain when you get here. Do you still have your bond to Oka?"

"Yes."

"Follow her to the valley of the crystal lake. I'm there. We're there." She kissed me again and then I was awake under the rock pile. Scrambling to my feet, I was off and running before I could really think straight. I was going to Pam.

I hit the porch of the farmhouse still running and shifted to two legs as I fell through the door with only pants on. Apparently I'd lost some of my ability to keep my clothes with me.

"I have to go." I was breathless and staring at Rylee sitting on the floor with Mars. Another toddler, blond-haired and blue-eyed, strode out of one room and pointed a finger at me.

"Zaps!"

An electrical zing snapped me in the ass. "Zane!" Rylee barked his name and he cringed.

"Sorry. He's new!"

"He's not new," Rylee muttered, giving me the stink eye, "just stubborn. And now he's running off again."

I rubbed at the sore spot. "I'm going to her, Rylee. I have to."

She rolled her eyes and I was surprised that she didn't yell at me. "You think you can keep her from being like Raven? You really believe that?"

I did believe it. "I think that love is strong enough, Rylee. Just like it was for you and me. But you don't need me anymore. You've got . . ." I swept my arm out to encompass everything here. "And she doesn't."

"She attacked three elementals last week," Rylee said. "Tore them apart. And there have been countless reports of supernaturals going missing. Not bad ones, Alex. Good people."

I wanted to counter that Pamela would never hurt

people without cause, but I couldn't be sure. And . . . I wasn't sure that I cared. "I'm going. I just, I couldn't leave without saying goodbye."

She stood and shooed the children out of the room. Then she came and took me by the hands. "Just remember, you were my wolf first." She winked and tugged me into a hug. "And that one day, she might not be the woman you love anymore."

I wanted to argue with her. But I knew she wasn't wrong.

I didn't take anything with me except for the knife I'd been given within the Veil all those years ago. I took off running, following the call of my pack. Of my girls.

And I couldn't stop the grin on my face.

Each day I got up before the sun and ran until I dropped. Eating and drinking only enough to keep me moving. I met a few supernaturals along the way.

They talked of a mountain witch who killed without care. Who took delight in death.

Who set things in motion that they didn't understand.

I blocked it out.

I kept running.

Three weeks passed. I heard that the human haven was strong and growing.

I'd gone to check on them after Pamela had left. Marley had stepped up and was helping Crimson, and Wade was running things alongside Dick. Who was still being a dick from time to time, apparently. Pamela had made that place, had given them safety, and it was a good thing. They called the central town Thornhaven.

I kept running.

Rumors of a succubus reached me, rumors that I was sure were my sister. I didn't detour. Maybe I would come back, but not today, not yet. My heart pulled me forward faster, and faster.

Three more weeks passed before I reached the edge of the mountains and began to climb. At the top of the first peak, I looked down into a valley with a crystalline lake, a blue so sharp and cold that I had no doubt this was the place. Across from the lake was a structure that could only be called a castle, built of stone.

In front of it, a tiger lazed.

"OKA!" I yelled her name and her head snapped around to face me. I ran around the side of the lake, dodging boulders and logs.

She met me part way, tackling me to the ground. "I knew you'd come!"

I hugged her tightly, even as awkward as it was. "Only a wolf would be able to make that journey. It's a good thing Pam didn't make you run it."

"Are you serious?" She pulled her head back, teeth bared. "You took six weeks! I could have done it in half that time."

I laughed and pushed to my feet. "She's here. Right?" A part of me was afraid I was wrong. That maybe Pam hadn't wanted me here.

"She's waiting in the library. Always in the library," she muttered. "Also, you are too skinny."

I shrugged. "Make me dinner then."

She took a mock swipe at me and I dodged her, hurrying toward the castle. Why a castle? Why couldn't Pam have come for me? Question after question rolled through my mind and then I was there, standing in front of the main doors to the castle. It looked vaguely familiar.

"Wait, is this the castle from the Veil?" I'd been there enough times, I knew what it looked like.

"Patterned after it," a man said. A man I knew. I slowly turned to see Raven looking back at me.

"How am I not surprised you aren't dead?" I growled. Wondering if I could kill him myself. "You did this to her."

"Actually, she embraced it, like the queen she is," he said softly.

"Queen?"

Her voice cut through it all. "Queen of Darkness."

I turned and she was there, in the same blue dress, her hair swept up into a loose pile of white curls, a few escaping their bonds. And the world just was . . . gone . . . all I could see was her. She turned and I followed her without a question.

She opened a set of doors and led me to what was the library. "Pam—"

"I go by Thorn now," she said softly. "That is the name my mother gave me. Pamela . . . I grew out of that name. How do you like the library?"

I clenched my hands to my sides, I wanted so badly to touch her. "I love you no matter what your name is." I paused and smiled. "The library reminds me of another."

She smiled. "The one in the Veil?"

My jaw dropped. "How did you know?"

Pam—no, Thorn—snapped her fingers and a coin danced across her knuckles. "I used this to go back and get information, old books and such. Fergus didn't want to let them go, but I convinced him."

In her eyes, was a flicker of darkness. "The witch—Sam—she's quiet for the most part. And she likes the incubus in you which makes this easier. She won't fight me having you here."

Another smile and then she stepped close. "Just love me, Alex, that's what I want. That's what I need."

"Always." I picked her up and kissed her, wishing we weren't in a damn library. I couldn't stop from touching her, I wanted—

"Hey," a soft little voice cut through the lust. "I remember you."

I pulled back from Pam to see Frost in the doorway. "I remember you too. You've grown up some."

He bobbed his head. "Yup, I'm a big guy now. Thorn, Wolf is awake."

She bobbed her head, her cheeks flushing. "We'll get him."

"Wolf?"

She took my hand and led me out of the library. "I needed to know you would come for me. Just for me."

A few doors down, she pushed open another door. A child's room.

A baby only a few months old was lying in a crib. Black hair, chubby little fists . . . and those eyes . . . one for each parent. One blue, one golden, staring back at us. Thorn bent and picked him up, holding him to her chest gently.

"This is our son, Alex."

27

THORN

"Did he believe you?" Oka asked me quietly as we walked the edge of the lake. Alex was playing with Wolf, loving him intensely already. I'd tweaked Alex's mind only a little, so that he believed any elemental blood he smelled on my son flowed from my heritage.

"Yes. He believes that is his son." Sorrow flickered through me. "I can't have another child, Oka. I can't give him the child he deserves, and Wolf will need the love of a father who is not a murderous bastard as his biological father was."

"I know. Sam would have a fucking heyday with that if she thought she could warp a child of an incubus too." She sighed. "But why bring Alex here then? You said you loved him enough to let him go."

I bit my lower lip. "Because there will come a day when I'm not strong enough, Oka. Not strong enough to battle off Sam. When I will go under the darkness. You and I both know that."

SHANNON MAYER

Sam laughed softly.

Truth.

My jaw flexed and I shoved the darkness down, wrapping Sam up so she could not hear my words, a trick I'd been working on the last year. "And when that day comes, my son will need a father strong enough to walk away, to take him from us." I put my hand on her head. "And both my boys will need a familiar to see them through."

"Not today," Oka grumbled. "That will be a thousand years from now, longer maybe."

I smiled at her as the sun broke through the clouds. "Not every villain knows they are the bad guy, Oka, but I do, and I know the role I need to play. To keep the elementals in check. To keep the demons fearful. To keep those who are strong on their toes. But you are right, that time is not today."

We stood in a patch of sunlight that warmed me through the thick clothing, but no further. I drew a deep breath in, wishing I could take the light into me, that I could banish the darkness.

Because one day I'd lose my fight with the shadows inside of me, but until then, I would hold all I loved dear.

And the world would be safer for that love because I took the crown and placed it on my own head.

Even if those I protected never knew the cost I willingly bore.

"A villain in name only," Oka said softly. "That's what no one will ever realize. The villain's story is never told. People always assume the worst, not knowing the lengths you will go to in order to protect them all."

I kept a hand on her. "But maybe this time will be

different. Maybe someone will tell our story and see the truth."

She snorted. "Please. What are you going to do? Hire some half-cut hack?"

I couldn't help the laugh that escaped me. "Be careful what you suggest, Oka. I might just do it."

One day my story would be told, and then they would know.

For the first time, the villain would be the hero.

I only wondered if I would still be myself when that day came.

28

RYLEE

"He's gone?" Liam asked me later that night when all the kids were tucked into bed and the night air had cooled off the late summer heat. The farm didn't feel the same without Alex, but there had been no holding him here.

"Yes. I think she spelled him. As unhappy as he was, he never once wanted to go to her until today," I said.

"We're going to have to deal with her, aren't we?" He sighed as he lay down beside me. He flinched and reached under the covers to pull out Marcella's wooden sword. He tossed it to the side and drew me against him.

"Yes, I think we are," I said softly. "She isn't our Pam anymore."

He nodded, yawned and closed his eyes. In seconds, he was out like a light.

"Must be fucking nice," I muttered. I pulled away from him, stood and walked through the house, checking on all those that were in my family now.

Out the front door into the coolness of the night, I made my way to the barn. "Eve."

The harpy turned her head toward me. Her children had flown away last year, and she was missing them terribly. "Rylee, is something wrong?"

I frowned. "I need to see Doran. Can you take me to him?"

She fluffed her wings and hopped forward. "We haven't been flying together in a long time. Why don't you want to take Ophelia?"

There was no jealousy there, not an ounce of it. Ophelia was a massive red dragon, bonded to me. "She's hardly incognito," I said dryly.

Eve laughed. "True enough."

I climbed onto her back, and she launched into the air. The wind blowing across my face felt good. Much as I loved my babies, I missed the freedom.

We flew for about two hours before Eve started to drop, landing in front of a perfectly blank space of land. "Still hiding?" I called out.

The air shimmered and a house and central yard appeared, adobe style. Doran had recreated what he'd had before the breaking of the world.

He strode out of the house, shirt off, piercings in his lip and nipples catching the little bit of light. Then again, I could see in the dark as well as any vampire, so there was that.

"Rylee. What are you doing here?"

"What do you think?" I tossed back.

He nodded. "Pamela? You want me to tell you what's

coming now that she's settled into her role as the Queen of Darkness?"

"Shit on a green stick," I whispered one of my cousin's favorite sayings. "Is that what she's calling herself?"

"Worse," he said softly. "That's what she *is*."

He paused and blew out a slow breath. "Because of what is coming, I can only put it one way."

I clenched my hands at my sides, wishing I had a sword there. "Tell me."

"Rylee," he looked me in the eyes, "we have a problem. And her name is Thorn."

AFTERWORD

Well that was a bit of a ride, wasn't it? I have to tell you, there were some shocks for me along the way, and I was the hack writing her story! ;)

So for those of you who've been with me and my worlds a little while, you can see where this is headed. A possible break back into Rylee's journey. Hang onto your panties, it won't be tomorrow. HA! But it seemed natural to swing back her way.

For those of you newer to me, don't worry, Pamela AHEM, Thorn, will still be around. But her part of the story will be different now.

I've always got lots going on in my writing worlds, and right now is no different. You can check out my "Shadowspell Academy" book which is coming out April 9th (co-written with KF Breene), and you can always see what's what on my website….

www.shannonmayer.com

OR sign up for my bitching not too often newsletter!

Newsletter